Ros

# Naisha Randhar

INDIA · SINGAPORE · MALAYSIA

# Notion Press Media Pvt Ltd

No. 50, Chettiyar Agaram Main Road,
Vanagaram, Chennai, Tamil Nadu – 600 095

First Published by Notion Press 2021
Copyright © Naisha Randhar 2021
All Rights Reserved.

ISBN 978-1-63940-347-9

*To my grandpa,*

*Thank you for everything.*

# ONE

**A scuffed piece of paper with messy,** quick words scribbled across it in uneven writing lay on the marble dinner table. With a hasty nod, a servant explained, "Your parents left zis for you. They asked that you read zit." A thick accent wove through his voice, an annoying effect of living in Atlantis, the underwater city, for the majority of his life. It made understanding him very difficult, but I was able to piece together the essence of what he uttered.

"They're gone again?" I asked, a stroke of disappointment brushing through my voice. "But they just got home. They promised we'd eat together." For once. My father's promising, loving smile that, yet again, had earned my trust, drifted through my head.

They lied.

*Again.*

"Unfortunately, zis fancy, upstage life does not come from nothing," the servant replied coldly, a tinge of jealousy lacing his voice, audible even through his accent. "They work, earn money. You're rich. This is how ze world works."

"Go polish a table or something," I snapped, glaring at him. The servant, scowling, strutted off stiffly with a rag swinging from his hand.

I stared after him, standing there for a few moments, wondering if I had it in myself to read the pitiful, apathetic note left on the table for me. Part of me didn't want to see what sorry excuse they'd made up this time, but the other part, some tiny fragment of me, wondered if this was different.. Maybe this letter would be different.

I forced myself to make my way to the table, trying to shove the icy memory of past broken promises.. One such memory still floated to the fore. I remembered how, more than five years ago, one night, they had promised to be back by eight. Instead, they left me a note saying that they would be gone for weeks. I tried to expel the conversation that I overheard from my mind, but the crushing moments replayed in my head, nonetheless.

"Won't Seamus be upset if we leave for Gryphon without him?" I heard my mother through the cracked, open space of the kitchen door, a silhouette of light shining on to the wooden floor.

"He'll be fine. The boy has to grow up someday," my father muttered.

"George, I'm worried he won't be okay. He will throw a fit when we tell him."

"It'll only be a few weeks. We can send him to Phoenix's house, Jane. He'll be fine."

"No, he won't. Even with Phoenix, he *hates* it when we aren't in town."

"You're right." There was a long pause. "Maybe it will be better to go without telling him."

I hardly remember seven-year-old me turning around, tears burning in my eyes, bolting up the stairs, throwing myself on to the bed and bursting into sobs. I hugged my knees as I cried into my sheets, wishing for the warmth of a family.

The memory stung.

Today seemed no different. The world seemed to have paused, and in a moment, I was standing in front of the table, my eyes fixed on the overturned note.

Finally, after a sigh, I flicked the paper over and frowned at the chicken scratch on the slip.

*Seamus,*

*We apologize. We will not be able to make it to dinner this evening. We have myriad things to sort out at work. There is sushi in the fridge from De Lacour—your favorite restaurant. We sincerely hope you enjoy the food.*

*Mom & Dad*

I didn't even like De Lacour. The irony of the situation was staring right out of the note. And, '*things to take care of at work*'? They could have at least cared enough to come up with a better excuse!

Anger burned through me white hot. I snatched the note off the table and ripped it to pieces furiously, letting the little fragments of paper rain on to the floor.

Why couldn't I have parents who cared? Who knew me? Parents who didn't just buy fancy stuff, but wanted me?

I stomped on the pieces of paper, kicking them into the air and letting them float around aimlessly.

"Really!" the same servant I had sent away huffed irritably, storming up to where I stood. "You could not zust leave zit there? So spoiled, so privileged—"

"Why don't we trade lives?" I spat angrily, clenching my fist. "I'm sure you'd enjoy being the spoiled, bratty twelve-year-old boy you've always wanted to be!"

Then I whirled around and raced through the halls, my footsteps echoing through the cavernous, empty chambers. It felt like it took me forever to reach the giant front doors that overlooked the entrance hall. I shoved myself against the thick wood to crack the door open enough to squeeze through. Then I took off, down the sloping front yard, darting through the streets, the only notion in mind being to get away from the forbidding, ripped apart note that still lay beneath the dinner table.

The road flew like fire under me. I bounded down the gravel and cut through the dead-grass field. I cantered through the thickening vegetation, pushing my way past scratchy branches and tumbling bushes.

"Phoenix!" I called into the opening. My voice rippled through the grass like waves. "Phoenix, where are you?"

The low hum of early crickets met my voice.

*"Phoenix! Come on, this isn't funny!"*

"Sorry!" a voice perked from beyond the layer of trees that shielded a wild, overgrown path I'd never ventured onto. "I'm over here!"

"Might want to be a bit more specific!" I called as I attempted to follow the trail of her voice beyond the thicket of trees. I trudged through the damp scenery. "Phoenix? You there?"

"There you are." Phoenix appeared next to me with a wide smile stretched across her face. "Why are you in such a huff? You're the one who's early."

"You're here early too," I pointed out, purposefully dodging her comment.

"I was exploring." Her voice dropped a bit, and I could detect a sense of sorrow thrumming through her tone. But it disappeared quickly, making way for her upbeat question: "Guess what I found!"

"What?" I followed her as she turned around and excitedly led me deeper into the woods.

"Look!" Phoenix pointed zealously to a huge cliff next to a field of glistening late blooms. "It overlooks the sea. The view is beautiful." Her eyes turned to me. "Come on, you've got to see it."

"Somebody's in a good mood," I commented, my spirits already rising as we staggered down the steep hill towards the cliff. I slid on to the grass as we reached the cliff, settling into a comfortable position to watch the sunset. Then I frowned. "Hey, you know there's a much easier way to get here, right?"

"Wow," Phoenix murmured, seeming not to have heard me, as she gazed out on to the vast sea; above it was a dazzling sunset that consisted of more colors than I could name. Strands of her wavy, brown hair wisped loose in the wind and sunlight danced across her caramel skin. "I can't believe I've never done this before."

Her neck tensed and her eyes widened. My words seemed to finally have sunk into her mind. She spun towards me, her amber eyes beaming golden in the sunset as she gave me an accusing look. "Seamus! How long have you known about this place? Why didn't you tell me about it?"

"There's a *way* easier path around the trail," I said, a laugh escaping my lips. I covered it up quickly after earning a deadly glare. "And the reason I never told you was because of this." When she gave me a perplexed look, I leaned in and explained, "I needed a place to save my ears from your nonstop chatter."

"Hey!" Phoenix elbowed my side. My face twisted into a scowl, but she turned back to the sunset. "My mom would kill me if she knew I snuck out," she mentioned casually. "I did this for you." She poked my arm.

I swatted her hand away, but grinned while I did. "I know," I said. After a second, I added, "Mary would kill me too, but she's taking another one of her two-hour baths." We both laughed loudly. The wind blew the long grass next to us sideways.

Mary has been my maid since I was born, but that doesn't mean I like her. Even though she knows my name is pronounced *Sea-mus*, not *Sha-mus*, like it's supposed to be pronounced, she says it the other way anyway. She's meant to watch me when my parents aren't around, which is basically always, but she usually has her own things to do.

Phoenix's laughter rang out across the sparkling water like she was speaking into a megaphone. The vibrancy of her voice made everything feel better.

"There's probably hippocampi under the surface," Phoenix hinted not so subtly, while squinting at the sea with her hands cupped over her eyes. "Remember when we saw two of them?"

"I remember," I agreed edgily, gandering at her. "But they rarely ever come above the surface. We just got lucky."

There was a moment of silence, yet I knew what Phoenix was thinking before she made an expression.

"No!" I shouted, springing up from the long grass. "I'm not jumping in!"

Phoenix grinned at me, not even bothering to deny her evil thoughts. "Why not? You can just make the water catch you if you're super scared. Neither of us have ability restrictors."

Many kids in Arma have a unique power, and mine is the ability over water. Most of them dwindle with age, but some become more powerful over time. Given the strength and the nature of my power, it was expected to become stronger. My training to control my power started when I was five, ever since I discovered it. Phoenix's power was also expected to grow. She found out about her power over fire a few months before me. We trained together since our elements are opposites, but since her power was so destructive and dangerous, she had to take many more lessons than me. We were not allowed to practice our powers outside lessons.

Some kids ignored that rule when out and about. That's why some parents bought their children ability restrictors—some seriously annoying magic that had been in vogue lately.

"For one, there could be a kraken down there for all we know! The Loch Ness monster might be living under that bay!"

Phoenix scoffed. "Don't be ridiculous. The Loch Ness monster lives in a lake. And we know *exactly* which one: the Loch Ness." She smirked.

"Don't be smart with me," I warned, backing up. "I'm not jumping!"

Phoenix crossed her arms with an irked look smeared across her face. "Stop being such a worrywart. Are you really scared of krakens in this bay? They live in deeper waters, which you should know. The only creatures beneath us are hippocampi and merpeople."

"Merpeople? Is that why you're doing this?"

"No... okay, maybe partially. But come *on*. We can swim to the beach straight after. You'll be falling for half a millisecond."

*"No!"* I cried, stepping backwards. "There's no way I'm jumping!"

"Why not?" Phoenix asked, as if it was a serious question.

Her eyes, flecked with gold, studied me.

She *was* being serious.

I bit my lip hesitantly. "Because..." I examined her carefully. "This is something I've never told anyone. Not even you."

"Obviously."

"I'm afraid of heights," I whispered quickly.

Phoenix stared at me. "You're afraid of *heights*?"

A mocking smile danced in her eyes.

"I know. It's stupid."

"But you like pegasus riding," stated Phoenix matter-of-factly.

I shrugged. "When I'm with River, it isn't as scary. I trust her. I know she won't let me fall. But actually jumping off a cliff?" I shook my head.

Phoenix placed a light hand on my shoulder. "You should've just said so, Seamus. Loads of people are afraid of heights. It's not exactly *rare*."

I blinked. "I'm not sure if that was supposed to be an insult or comforting."

"Consider it both."

*"Phoenix!"* I shouted. That's when she took off, tearing through the fields that were blossoming with flowers. I bolted after her, swinging my arms to dodge the swaying grass. *"PHOEENIXXXX!"*

\*\*\*

The next morning when I woke up, a crashing rumble of thunder greeted me. I stayed in bed underneath the silky covers, staring at the canopy above me, wondering why it had to be raining. No pegasus riding today, that was for sure. But then I remembered that Phoenix had begged me to search for unicorns in the woods that bordered my house. I had rolled my eyes and said, *"Girls."* I knew we'd be going anyway. That was just how Phoenix was..

There was a loud knock on my door. Scrambling to my feet and snatching some clothes to appear decent, I yelled, "Who is it?"

"It's me, Seamus," came the voice of my mom. "I need to talk to you. Can you meet me downstairs in five minutes?"

The tone of her voice made me feel sick. "Why?"

It was too late. I heard her footsteps already making their way through the long halls and echoing down the stairs until they were entirely inaudible. I waited for a minute, my ear cocked to the door, until I was sure she was gone. Then I circled back to my bed, which was very messy—with clothes sprawled across the sheets and books scattered throughout the comforters—pondering what caused the melancholy to enter my mom's voice.

Five minutes later, I was heading down the grand marble staircase, past huge, decorative windows that peered down on to the vast courtyard in front of my house. It took me a while to get down, considering how long they were. Some days, I feel like they've grown.

"Seamus." Mom sat in the kitchen, her hands cupped around a coffee mug. Her black hair was mussed up and her eyes full of concern, which made me uneasy. She gestured towards the chair next to her. "Sit."

It sounded like I'd regret it.

Still, I dropped down next to her and glanced at my dad, whose hands lay crossed on the table. He eyed my mom in a strange way.

"Look, Seamus, there's something we need to tell you." Dad stole a look at Mom hesitantly, then moved his attention back to me. He heaved a huge breath. "I'm going away."

"Away?" I blinked.

*This* was the big deal?

Mom brought me downstairs to tell me Dad was going on another trip?

"You're gone most of the time. What's the big deal?" I said with a joking smile, reaching to grab a plate of pancakes from the table.

"No, you don't understand, son. I'm leaving. For good." Dad side-eyed Mom nervously, who nodded and carefully studied her feet. "I'll come back to visit, though."

*"Visit?"* I sputtered, whipping my hand back as realization swept over my senses and the pieces began to fit together. "What do you mean *visit*?"

"He's going to cross the Bridge to Calica tomorrow," Mom intervened hastily, obviously realizing that my father was not doing a great job explaining.

A wave of anger and betrayal pierced me like a dagger.

"He's going to the other *queendom*?"

Mom glared at Dad scornfully, who shifted towards me. "I want to start over. Try again."

"Start over? What do you mean, *start over*?" I gasped, panic destroying my equanimity. The words hit me like fists punching my stomach.

My dad.

My *own* dad.

Leaving me.

I gaped at him, trying to process his words. "I thought, in your heart, you loved us!"

"I *do*. I mean, I love you, and your mother, very much…"

Mom let out a funny noise.

Dad gave her a *you're-not-helping* look. He turned his attention to me. "Look, son, we just need to be apart for a while. Your mom and I have a few things to work out."

"You mean you're getting divorced," I stormed.

It wasn't a question.

Dad began to look uncomfortable. "Well, I mean, nothing's for sure yet—"

"I don't believe it. I really don't believe it!"

"Look, son—"

"How long has this been going on? How long have you been planning to divorce?"

Dad gulped. "I'm not sure."

"You aren't *sure*?"

"Maybe a few months," Mom answered quietly, carefully inspecting her hands in her lap.

"A few *months*?"

Mom didn't hesitate. "Six."

"Six?" I asked, a bad taste forming in my mouth. I let out a shaky breath. My knees felt sore, and my eyes stung. Everything seemed unfocused.

*Six months.*

"I'm sorry," Mom whispered, resting her hand on mine. "I'm really, really sorry, Seamus."

I shook her hand off and stood up, glaring at both of them. "So that's it? You've been planning this for six months and you only tell me the day before? You're just going to leave tomorrow? No more family game nights? No more pegasus riding? No more fantasy stories about the Forbidden Seas?"

"We didn't do those things much," Mom interceded almost pleadingly.

"Sure, you never have any time for me, but at least we were a family!"

"I'm desperately trying here—" Dad started.

"And desperately failing," I interrupted coldly. "I would know." Then I stomped out, leaving my parents stunned.

***

I stared at the ceiling of my room, watching the reflections of the water droplets raining down outside dance across the ceiling while feeling wretched.

My parents were getting *divorced.*

Was it stupid to be angry? Was I being cold and unreasonable towards my parents, or the other way around?

What if I really was just a spoiled, bratty twelve-year-old boy? Thoughts bulleted through my head, leaving a painful, cold wasteland of dead love in their wake.

*When have they ever actually had time for me? When have they remembered one of my pegasus riding practices or picked me up from school? They never even sat down and ate dinner with me. They're away all the time, sometimes not coming back for weeks, or even months. They never really cared for me..*

I closed my eyes when I realized how horribly honest these words were. Before I could brood over the heart-wrenching truth of this, a muffled sound caught my attention.

*THUD!* My eyes traveled to the window as I frowned. *THUD!* A rock catapulted in a wobbly arc and hit the glass pane of my window. It wasn't hard to guess who it was.

*Seriously?* Couldn't she forget about her stupid unicorns?

Scowling, I made my way to the window. As soon as I managed to wrench it open, a tiny pebble arched through the window and caught me in my chest.

*"Phoenix!"* I thundered, rubbing my chest.

"Sorry!" Her familiar voice chirped from below me.

I leaned out the window. Sure enough, Phoenix peered up at me with a pack at her side, soaked from head to toe, but grinning. Rain sprinkled towards the ground and left droplets dripping from the mountainous pine trees.

A knot in my stomach sucked up all my happiness. Couldn't she just leave me alone?

"What do you want?" I called down.

Phoenix's grin disappeared. She looked shocked, I felt bad. So I yelled, "Come on up."

"From here?" Surprise took over her face.

"Where else?"

Phoenix blinked. "Um, okay."

She grasped a low branch on the tree outside my window and hoisted herself up. Then she grabbed another branch and swung herself around. She repeated the process over and over again until she was finally right next to my window. Grinning, she climbed in.

"Hi," she greeted, standing up and brushing herself off.

I gazed at her, but the words got stuck in my throat. I swallowed and tried again. "Hi," I responded quietly.

She frowned at me. "What's up with you today?"

"What's that supposed to mean?"

"You realize that when you say that, I know you know *exactly* what I mean?" Phoenix raised an eyebrow and flopped down in my chair. "Spill."

I turned away, frustration and anger building up inside me like a toddler stacking building blocks. The tower swayed left and right, about to spill all over the ground, leaving emotion splattered everywhere and a huge mess that someone would need to clean up.

Probably me.

"My parents are getting divorced," I mumbled.

"Oh, yeah, sure."

The escalade of emotion crashed right on Phoenix's head.

I whirled around angrily. "I'm serious! My dad's crossing the Bridge to Calica tomorrow—and he's not coming back!"

I glowered at her furiously, breathing hard, and then I sat down, my legs crossed. "Sorry," I growled, though I didn't feel sorry. I wished I could punch a bunch of holes in the wall.

"Seamus…" Phoenix studied me. Her eyes filled to the brim with concern and worry. "I'm sorry."

"Me too."

She considered me carefully before placing her hand on mine. I pulled away, the hoodie I was wearing covering my eyes. She looked down, but I didn't need to see her to know there was hurt seeping through her eyes.

I didn't know what else to do.

I shouldn't be angry at Phoenix. But the uncontrollable hurricane of emotion inside me blasted without reason.

Before, I could tell Phoenix anything. But now, I just wanted to be alone. Right now, there was a canyon-sized chasm between me and the rest of the world.

I glanced at Phoenix. I could tell she wasn't sure what to say.

I gave her a small smile. "Thanks," I murmured. She nodded, and I peeled my eyes away from her, feeling small in a really big world. A world that didn't care what I had to say. Even my parents wouldn't listen to me. No one would, except Phoenix. The difference between Phoenix and my parents was that she would never leave me to go to the other side of the world. She'd always be by my side.

Always.

I sucked in a huge breath, thoughts spinning like thread in my head along with the moment when my parents admitted they were getting divorced replaying over and over again like a recording. "Can I ask you something?"

Phoenix studied me and nodded. "Anything."

Anything is a big word. When people say anything, they usually don't really mean *anything*.

But Phoenix did.

I could see it in her eyes. She wanted to help me.

I surveyed her carefully before dropping my eyes to the ground, the courage stacked up inside me now melting away. Before it was completely gone, I asked in a small voice, "Are you happy?"

I really hoped she didn't know where I was going.

*I* wasn't even sure where I was going.

Was I?

Phoenix creased her eyebrows, her eyes contemplating my expression. "That's a weird question," she remarked, watching me with penetrating eyes. I forced my eyes to stay on her, trying to stay calm while waiting for an answer. She shrugged, but her facial features tensed with suspicion. "Sure. It's always been fun around here with you to keep me company."

"What if I wasn't here?"

Uh-oh.

Phoenix stood up with clenched fists. "You aren't thinking of moving to Calica with George, are you?"

I shook my head, wondering if I should go on.

"Then what?" She glared at me. Her laser eyes bored through my mind, but I shook my head again.

"Just answer the question," I mumbled, cursing myself for opening my big mouth about it.

She watched me for a moment, waiting for more.

When I remained silent, she put her hands on her hips impatiently. "If you leave, I'll be really mad. So mad I might hunt you down and kill you."

A weak chuckle escaped me. "Is that a threat?"

"Only if you fear dying."

Then, in a moment, solemness settled over me as I remembered what was at stake. I stared at Phoenix and whispered, "I'm running away."

# TWO

**"Running away?" Phoenix gaped at me,** appalled. "What do you mean, running away?"

She dropped down, shaking her head in disbelief as the color drained away from her face. Her eyes fixed on me with shards of worry and fear scattered inside them. "No, Seamus, you have to be serious with me here. You aren't kidding? You're running away?"

I nodded.

Phoenix puffed out a breath. "You really want me to hunt you down and kill you, don't you?" She tried desperately.

It sounded like it was supposed to be a joke, but her tone threw daggers at me. When Phoenix got like that, I knew I had to wade carefully.

Fear churned in my stomach to reveal the heart-stopping sentence my mind stayed stuck on.

"No," I admitted, looking down. "I'd like you to join me."

Phoenix goggled at me, a look mixed with sympathy and incredulity plastered across her face. "*Join you*? Running away? Away where? Away to that old shed down in Gilmo?"

I bit my lower lip with trepidation pounding through me. "I'm going much farther away than to another city." I hesitated. "I want to go to Calica."

Phoenix gawked at me, her face paling, but seeing the expression on my face, she had the gumption to ask, "Why?"

"I don't know!" I rose from the ground, my vision blurred, wishing she would stop asking so many questions. "I don't have any plans! I just want to go somewhere far away from here."

"But… George… George will be in Calica."

I cringed.

"Fine." I gritted my teeth. "I'll go to the Bridge. I'll travel the Forbidden Seas." I knew I sounded stupid. The Forbidden Seas is the body of water between and surrounding the two kingdoms of Arma, Calica and Timnock. But it's highly dangerous, and even though there are protection spells near the shore, people are always warned never to approach the waters. "I'll go *somewhere.* I'll go *anywhere* but here!"

Phoenix studied me carefully. I waited for a minute, preparing for the sharp, two-letter word that was undoubtedly coming my way—NO! Phoenix *had* a family. A perfectly happy family that always had time for her. If she came with me, she'd lose her family, her home, and all her friends. Other friends. The better offer here was painfully obvious.

"You really want to go?" Phoenix asked quietly, lacing her fingers together so hard that her knuckles turned white.

I hesitated for a moment, but nodded.

She took a deep breath. "Let me pack my bag."

"I… really?" I gasped.

Phoenix reached out and hugged me tightly. When she pulled away, her eyes were moist, but her expression was determined. "We're best friends, Seamus. Best friends do everything together. They'd do anything for each other. Either way, I have no doubt that you'd do it for me."

"What should I pack?" she started uneasily. "Food? Money? How many liens?"

"A *lot*," I advised, my spirits rising with my hope. "In fact, bring your entire savings."

"My *entire* savings?"

"Would you rather leave it here?" I pointed out.

"Good point," Phoenix agreed, but she looked grave. Her eyes were glazed over, and her face unusually colorless. Instantly, I felt bad. This was a lot to ask from a friend, even one like Phoenix. Not to mention, one look at her face and you would think I'd asked her to journey to Cerem, the island where the most dangerous monsters of Arma crept.

"Look, if you don't want to go, I get it," I assured Phoenix, despite the growing lump in my throat. "I really do. This is a lot to ask. I wouldn't blame you for saying no." I closed my eyes, wishing the hollowness inside me would diminish. "In fact, I'd blame myself if you said yes." My hopes were already sinking, but I didn't have a choice. For extra assurance, I added, "What kind of friend asks their best friend to do something like this?"

The worst best friend, that's who.

Phoenix viewed me for so long, I wondered if she'd fallen asleep, until she announced, "I'm going to come. I'm going to come, and that's that. No more talk about it."

I peeked up at her. "Are... are you sure?"

"Of course, I am!" Phoenix looped her arm into mine with enthusiasm that was very obviously forced. "I mean, we have my entire savings and yours. It'll probably get us far. We could work as magicians or something to earn money when we reach wherever we're going. And anyway, we've always wanted to be explorers. This might be our chance."

"If you're completely sure…" I said doubtfully, examining her carefully.

"I'm positive," Phoenix swore. "When are we doing it?"

Before I could answer, loud stomps and a ringing knock at my door made me jump. Seconds later, my mom's voice called, "Seamus? Who are you talking to?"

I inhaled sharply, and Phoenix cast a nervous glance at the door. Phoenix wasn't allowed to climb into my room through the window. She wasn't even allowed to *be* in my room, except on weekends, but of course, we never followed that rule.

"*Climb out the window! Fast!*" I mouthed.

She gazed at the window and stole a look back at me, nodding. Gingerly, she stood from her spot on my carpet and crept towards the window, clambering out as gracefully as she could without making a sound.

Then, realizing we hadn't decided when we'd do it, I yelled out of desperation, "*Tonight!*"

"Seamus?" Mom called again. "Phoenix better not be in there!"

"So what if she is?" I retorted, even surprising myself.

Since when did I become so snarky?

Still, I wished I had kept my mouth shut. I could almost feel the anger radiating off my mom like a volcano ready to explode. "I'm still your mother, mister!" Mom thundered. She swung open the door to find me sitting on the floor innocently, louring at her.

"Who were you talking to?" Mom demanded.

"I don't know what you're talking about," I lied, beginning to enjoy the moment.

Her eyes traveled to the open window and back to me.

Praying that Phoenix had already made it down, I wondered why I cared since I'd be gone tonight.

She whisked to the window, and I stayed where I was, my insides lurching as I tried to keep an impassive face. I watched her lean out and carefully examine every single blade of grass until she was finally able to conclude that Phoenix was not there.

I breathed a sigh of relief when she turned back to me.

"Phoenix was here, wasn't she?" Mom shot. "She came up through the window, didn't she? You *lied* to me. Tell me the truth!"

"Are you really in a position to yell at me?" I asked sweetly.

Okay, I seriously needed someone to cover my mouth.

"Yes, I am, since I'm your mother!"

And that's when I lost it.

"If you cared about me, cared at all, you would've convinced Dad to stay! You would've told him when he said he wanted to leave, 'Suck eggs! I won't let you do that to Seamus!' Or you should've at least told me earlier if you had this whole thing planned for *six months*!" I bellowed. Then I whirled away, out of breath. I wished I could scream into a pillow after beating the stuffing out of it.

Mom stared at me, stunned. I'm not exactly sure what she was thinking, but the next thing she said was, "I'm sorry, Seamus." Slightly taken aback, I realized her eyes were slightly wet. "I'm really sorry. We never meant to hurt you. I know we've made mistakes, but—"

"Sorry won't fix anything!" I snapped, ire flaring inside me. She didn't say anything. Unsure what to do, I glared at her. "Well?"

She just looked at me. "Do you want dinner served up in your room tonight?" she asked.

*She wants me to cool off,* I realized.

Well, fat chance.

I scowled at her, my emotions trapped inside of me. "Yeah, as a matter of fact, I would." She got up to leave, and just as she reached the door, I called, "And don't send Mary!"

Then she was gone.

Once I heard her footsteps fade away, I wondered, uneasily if I'd gone too hard on her. Maybe I could have been more understanding.

I probably could have.

I *definitely* could have. Divorce wasn't exactly uncommon. Neither could it have been easy on her.

Even if I was sorry, it wasn't like it mattered anymore. It was too late to take it back. I was leaving tonight, so if she hated me, she'd never have to see me again.

Never again. The two words were ice cold.

My window still hung loosely open, letting in a chilling breeze and allowing droplets of water to fly through. Luckily, I didn't hurry over there, because when I sauntered to close it, a paper airplane zipped through it, landing softly on my bed. Frowning, I reached down and unfurled it. Words were scribbled across it in familiar handwriting. I grinned, the comfort of Phoenix's friendship surrounding me when I saw what it read:

### Midnight

\*\*\*

The clock ticked fifteen minutes to twelve. Emotions swirled inside me. I was positioned in a crouch, my ear pressed to the door. Dressed in a warm sweater and sweatpants, I strained my ears for the smallest of sounds. Usually, I went to bed much earlier than my parents, so I had no idea if they were asleep or not.

Impatiently, I waited for something to break the pin-drop silence of the house. The loud slam of a bedroom door indicated that my parents had retired for the night.

*Deep breath.*

From here on out, my life would never be the same.

This was the biggest, most perilous decision of my life, yet I was sure I had to leave.

I eyed my watch, realizing I only had eight minutes left before my rendezvous with Phoenix.

Experienced with being light on my feet from the countless times I had sneaked out to see Phoenix, I quietly slid open the door and peered into the hallway. With an uneven piece of tape, I stuck a note to my door that read, *Sleeping in late. Need some time alone.* It was pretty believable, considering the scene I had put up with Mom.

As quietly as I could manage, I crept down the marble hallway with my pack slung around my shoulder.

Going faster now, I edged into the kitchen and eyed the money drawer. *Don't think of it,* I told myself in warning. *I have already packed my savings. Twenty-five liens, plus Phoenix's liens, is enough.* So instead, I turned my attention to food and snatched as many packs of snacks as I could carry without falling over.

Somehow, with my now bulging, seemingly one-hundred-pound pack, I managed to stagger to the front door and push it open.

"Finally!" Phoenix remarked. She was wielding a large pack as well, with running shoes, pants, and a cozy tunic on. "I was starting to think this was one of your pranks."

"Did you bring everything?"

"Yes." Phoenix patted her pack with satisfaction. "Are we ready to get going now?"

"Wait." I inspected Phoenix closely. "Thank you."

Phoenix grinned. "What are best friends for except to run away together? Know what I mean?" She winked.

A smile tugged at the corners of my mouth. "We need to get somewhere private."

Phoenix rolled her eyes and snorted. "Obviously."

"If it's so obvious, you should have ideas."

Phoenix smirked. "I do, in fact. Remember our old tree house? The one by Olin creek?"

The tree house was years old. We had asked our parents to build it for us when we found that all best friends have tree houses, but it didn't take long for us to tire of it.

"Oh, yeah," I replied sheepishly. "I forgot about that."

"Of course, you did."

***

"What have you got?"

Phoenix dumped the contents of her backpack on the peeling paint of the treehouse that now smelled of old bird food. "My entire savings—twenty-eight liens, a por for luck, clothes, food…"

I poured my things next to hers. "*My* entire savings, which is twenty-five liens." Phoenix raised an eyebrow complacently. I ignored her. "Food, more food, even more food, clothes…"

"Wow!" Phoenix's eyes bulged. "And I thought *I* overpacked."

My face tinged red. "Whatever."

"No, seriously," Phoenix persisted. "How are you going to carry this? You can't walk a mile with that pack weighing you down."

"I—"

Before I could respond, Phoenix interrupted. "So, where are we going anyway? I know you can't choose, but we have to go somewhere. It's not like we can live on the Bridge. So, choose. Calica or Timnock? Or are you planning on staying in Arma at all? We could go to another planet," she suggested.

"Tempting, but no. We'll live in one of the Bridge cities, so we might as well go there. Who knows? Maybe we'll figure it out on the way."

It wasn't really much of a plan.

The Bridge cities were the cities that were on either side of the Bridge. One is in Timnock, the other in Calica. Bridge cities were considered independent ports, not governed by either of the queendoms.

She surveyed me and nodded. I cast my eyes at her, incredulous at her tolerance, when she mentioned, "Well, we can't use River, since she injured herself last week. So, are we going to spend the night here and plan how to get to the Bridge tomorrow morning?"

"Nah," I said with a slight grin. "I have a plan."

# THREE

**"Where are we going?"** Phoenix whispered apprehensively. I didn't ask why she was whispering. We were out in the vast, empty woods that surrounded my house—the Olin woods. Phoenix and I used to dream of adventuring out there at night, even though our parents refused to let us. Now that we were actually doing it, I wondered why we had ever wanted to.

"I know a friend," I said in an undertone, wishing she'd be quiet. It was hard enough walking through deep, scary woods without someone talking incessantly beside you. It was basically an alarm that howled to all the monsters, *COME AND GET ME!*

Fortunately, Phoenix didn't ask more about the friend. Unfortunately, she didn't shut up. "It feels like we're on Cerem," she murmured. "I've always imagined what Cerem would be like, and it's like we're stepping foot there now."

Cerem was an island in the Forbidden Seas. It was a prison to almost all the monsters in the world, but some still roamed free. Alexander the Great (the founder of Arma and every kid's hero) imprisoned the monsters in Cerem, and was martyred.

"*Maybe*, if we were quieter, the monsters here would leave us alone," I hissed, giving her a dirty look. She didn't say anything.

After ten minutes of trudging through the deep, dark woods, we finally reached a fork in the road. I sighed with relief. "Finally," I whispered. "It shouldn't be long now."

"What shouldn't be?"

"His house," I replied, waving a hand at her. "The stables."

"Stables? Stables for what?"

"Pegasi," I stated, chancing a glance over my shoulder timidly. "Once I saw a brown pegasus flying over the woods, landing near here. I followed it, and that's when I found his house. He's got huge stables of pegasi. It's fantastic."

"*He?*"

"Mr. Koren," I responded quickly, picking my way through the wild brush. "He raises pegasi. It's what he does."

"So how will he help us?"

I rolled my eyes at that. "Isn't it obvious?"

Phoenix's eyes widened with eager glints sparkling inside them. "*Oh*! Are we really—"

A loud crunch stamped behind us. My eyes widened as I glanced at Phoenix, who motioned for me to crouch down. She stole a look at me, terrified. I knew exactly what she was thinking. Only one word echoed through our minds: *Monsters!*

My heart raced as I tried not to imagine what would happen if we ran into a monster. Holding my breath, my eyes stayed on Phoenix, but I focused my hearing on the woods. Our breathing echoed in my ears like an earthquake. It's strange how noisy a place can become if you really listen.

Out of nowhere, we heard a shout and a strangled cry.

"Monsters!" Phoenix hissed, clutching my hand.

This time, though I wished I could have made fun of her and laughed, I feared Phoenix was right. I looked at her with trepidation. "Should we go check it out?" I barely whispered.

All my instincts screamed not to. Every particle inside me told me we needed to whirl around and bolt.

It *was* a dumb idea. I was really hoping Phoenix would shake her head in a petrified way and we'd spend the rest of the night at the treehouse, me making fun of Phoenix's cowardice.

Unfortunately, she nodded. We locked eyes. Slowly, with bated breath, we stood up and peeked over the brush.

There, tangled in the middle of all the thorns and bushes that rounded the woods, was an abnormally large man. He had a badly trimmed beard and glasses with one lens shaped like a square and the other a circle. He wore pull-up overalls and a striped shirt underneath with hiking boots laced on his feet. Next to him was a small pistol, also entangled in the thorny vines that encased him. He struggled to grab on to something that could pull him out. It must've been really dark because when he saw us, he screamed and struggled harder than ever to seize his pistol.

Phoenix looked deeply shaken. "Seamus, run!" she shrieked.

"No, wait!" I grabbed her hand as she tried to bolt. She stared at me like I was crazy and pointed at the gun with fear in her eyes.

"He's going to shoot us if we stay!"

I spoke slowly, trying to calm her down. "He won't hurt us. This is Mr. Koren, the pegasus tender."

"Seamus?" Mr. Koren's raspy voice called out. "Is that you?"

Phoenix glanced at him, then back at me. "How do you know he won't sell us out?"

"Because he doesn't care about anyone except himself," I explained restlessly. "But he might not help us at all if we don't untangle him!"

"Seamus?"

Phoenix eyed him exasperatedly and said in a hushed tone, "So, *specifically*, how is he going to help us?"

"We will buy a pegasus from him."

Phoenix still seemed unconvinced.

She gazed back at Mr. Koren, who was struggling very hard to get untangled. Impatience bucked inside me like a restless horse. Sighing, she agreed.

We tramped back to Mr. Koren. He glimpsed me standing over him and frowned at me oddly. Or, maybe it wasn't an odd look. Everything seemed weird about Mr. Koren when he wore his glasses.

"Seamus? Is that you?"

Phoenix shook her head. I couldn't exactly blame her for not taking to Mr. Koren, but I gave her a look through the brush. Then I turned back to Mr. Koren, who looked disheartened.

"I'm here, Mr. Koren."

"Oh, thank goodness," Mr. Koren's relieved voice called. "I was sure I'd be stuck here forever. I heard a noise outside my house, so I came out to investigate, but then I tripped and landed myself here."

He brought a pistol to investigate a *noise*? Jeez, what does this guy deal with on a daily basis?

I crouched down to examine the knots Mr. Koren had tangled himself in. "These are too tight to be taken out by hand. Do you have anything that we could—"

"I have pliers in my pocket," Mr. Koren said. "I can't reach them. You're going to have to get them yourselves."

I glanced at Phoenix for help, but she conveniently pretended to be unaware. Rolling my eyes, I leaned in, searching for the pliers. I spotted them in Mr. Koren's left pocket. Phoenix watched as I cut the vines and branches that ensnared Mr. Koren. Finally, after almost twenty minutes of hard work, cutting each vine, I pulled Mr. Koren to his feet. He stood and brushed himself off. Then he peered at me from beneath his glasses with a smile stretched across his face.

"Thank you, Seamus," he acknowledged. He turned to Phoenix. "Introduce me to your friend now, will you?"

"Of course," I agreed. "Mr. Koren, this is Phoenix." I sent Phoenix a side-eye that said, *Be good.* She shrugged.

"Pleasure to meet you, Phoenix." Mr. Koren held out his hand. Phoenix, a bit hesitant, took it unenthusiastically.

"Pleasure to meet you as well," she muttered. "So… you sell pegasi, right? We wanted to buy one."

"Of course, of course!" Mr. Koren said, his eyes gleaming, as if those were his favorite words to hear. "I'm sure you'd find interest in one of them."

Phoenix nodded. "Sure, we will," she agreed a bit sarcastically.

"Follow me to my humble home," Mr. Koren offered. "It's quite small, but very comfortable. I'm sure I could fix you up something to eat, for your trouble." He dipped his head respectfully. "Are you going on a trip with your pegasus tonight?"

"Yeah," Phoenix answered as we followed him through the entangling greenery of the forest.

"Well, then, do you have any food for your journey?" Mr. Koren asked.

"We have a lot," I blurted before I could stop myself.

"Yeah, did you not notice Seamus's exploding pack?"

Mr. Koren chuckled humorously, but my glare shot daggers at Phoenix.

"Would you like my soup? I have thick bowls that's made of a special material that'll keep it warm for longer. I'm sure it would be very useful for your journey," Mr. Koren tried. I was muddled for a moment, unsure why Mr. Koren, the cheapest man I knew, would offer us anything for *free* except for cookies (they were complimentary), until he added, "I won't charge much."

That cleared everything up.

I decided not to mention that we didn't need any special material since Phoenix powered over fire. Not only that, but what Mr. Koren called quality was likely a piece of crumbling clay.

"No thanks, we're fine," Phoenix said, picking her way through the snatching vines and rustling brush with difficulty.

"Well, if you're sure…"

"What I really want to know is how much it takes to buy a pegasus?"

"Twenty liens," Mr. Koren answered automatically.

"Hmmm," Phoenix responded casually, raising an eyebrow at me.

After more long minutes of trudging through the dense forest, Mr. Koren finally led us to a little home that I would have mistaken for a toolshed at first glance. Its shutters were nearly falling off, its bricks were crumbling and decorated with moss, and the roof patching near the short chimney was nearly toppling over. Not just that, but he was absolutely right when he said it was small. The tiny house was smaller than my kitchen. No, not *my* kitchen. My parents' kitchen.

Ugh.

The thought of home made me sick. I wished for my warm bed, silky covers, and a good, hearty breakfast. But I pushed those thoughts away. There was no way I was going back now. We'd already embarked on our journey.

Phoenix and I followed Mr. Koren into his house. Mr. Koren insisted we sit down while he got the pegasi ready. There wasn't much place to sit down, except for a beat up old couch, but we sat down, nevertheless.

"Thanks," Phoenix said.

Mr. Koren wore a pleased expression. "No problem." He smiled. "Would you like some cookies? I just made them."

"As a matter of fact, that'd be really nice," Phoenix agreed, grinning.

Mr. Koren left to fetch cookies.

As we waited, I reached into my pack and took the map out. I unfurled it and laid it down on the coffee table in front of us. "So, we're in Jade, Timnock right now." I circled the dot marked *Jade* with a pen I found nearby. "If we were to leave Timnock and go to Calica, then we'd have to cross the Bridge. Either that, or cross the Forbidden Seas, which sounds ominous." I pointed at the drawing of a bridge marked *The Bridge*. "We'd have to go through our Bridge city, Leon, and then to Calica's Bridge city, Lilak." Bridge cities were cities on either side of the Bridge. "We're definitely going to the Bridge cities, so our ultimate destination right now is Leon." I drew an arrow from Jade to Leon. "We'll fly there." I looked up at Phoenix, smirking. "I think you already figured that part out."

Phoenix snorted. "Obviously."

"We'll have to make stops along the way, since pegasi can't fly that far continuously. We'll spend the night in each city until we're at Leon. Once we're there, we can figure out if we're gonna stay in Timnock or Calica." I leaned back. "That's all I've got."

Phoenix shrugged. "Good enough for me."

Mr. Koren strode into the room, balancing a platter full of freshly baked oatmeal cookies. "Here we are," he announced, placing the tray of cookies on the coffee table. "Hot and fresh."

"Fantastic." Phoenix licked her lips. She put one whole cookie in her mouth and picked a couple more. Greedy! Then she turned to Mr. Koren. "Would you mind showing us those pegasi now?"

"Not at all," Mr. Koren replied agreeably. He led us out the backdoor and across a large field of grass. "This is where my horses graze," he explained as we trudged across the field, round the trees. Soon a small, rectangular building appeared just ahead. "There they are—my stables."

I glanced eagerly at Phoenix, expecting her to be excited, but she frowned a bit.

I was beginning to get annoyed at her aloof attitude towards Mr. Koren.

Mr. Koren noticed, too, and beads of sweat appeared on his forehead. I let out a breath. Maybe Phoenix was smarter than I gave her credit for. Acting haughty might get us a better deal.

He fumbled with the key, but managed to insert it in and twist it. Then he pulled the doors open. My eyes widened and my mouth twisted into a grin when I saw all the pegasi lined up, one after the other, each of them more beautiful than the last.

"Wow," I breathed. I straightened up, trying to look cool. Fortunately, Mr. Koren had fixed his eyes on Phoenix, waiting for a reaction.

"They're beautiful." Phoenix gave an aloof smile.

Mr. Koren looked eager. "Choose your pick." Then he leaned in and whispered, "And trust me, I know this is the only place to get *quality* pegasi for cheap."

He said that like they were mere products on the market. But pegasi were beautiful, spirited creatures—forever companions.

Phoenix stepped into the stables and began inspecting the pegasi. She stopped at every stable, stroking them and whispering things I couldn't hear. Under her wavy hair, I could see a sneaking smile, and when she stopped at a stall with a small, stout pegasus, I knew she was as excited as I was. She reached out to stroke it fondly, her eyes shining. It neighed softly, and she beamed.

"What a small pegasus," she remarked, hiding her smile. She turned to Mr. Koren. "Can you give him to me for a discount? Considering how small he is, I mean."

"Ah, yes, of course," Mr. Koren agreed, a bit disgruntled. "I'll take, eh, say, eight liens off."

"So that'd be twelve liens in total?" Phoenix confirmed, pulling out her money bag.

Phoenix rummaged around her bag and came out a minute later with twelve coins in her hand. "This should cover it."

"Hmm." Mr. Koren frowned at the liens like he was wondering if they were real, but in the end, he took them in his hand and clasped them in his money pouch. "Thank you. It has been a pleasure doing business with you." He bowed respectfully.

Phoenix nodded, but shot me a vexed look.

Mr. Koren straightened up. "Let me take you to the carriages," he suggested.

Phoenix agreed as she took the pegasus out of his stable. The pegasus was dark brown and short, with deep, black eyes. Phoenix gazed at the pegasus, and warmth radiated off her. I stared at her with surprise as she said, "Aww, what's his name?"

"His name is Sorin," I replied when Mr. Koren didn't answer because he was too busy counting money. "Mr. Koren told me the last time I visited." I winked at Mr. Koren.

Phoenix stared at Sorin. "I get why you love pegasi so much, Seamus. You can just look into a pegasus's eyes and..." Her voice trailed off and her cheeks tinged red.

I grinned smugly. "Told ya they're great."

Phoenix handed Mr. Koren one jin as a tip. "Thank you for your service," she told him politely.

"Of… course…" Mr. Koren was still counting the liens for what was probably the tenth time.

"Can Sorin pull a carriage by himself?" Phoenix asked.

"Yes," I responded.

Mr. Koren led us to the carriages, still with a dazed expression on his face, clutching the money pouch tightly in his hand, probably wondering how he had got talked into giving an eight lien discount. Two carriages lined up next to each other. Phoenix, who led Sorin, hooked Sorin on to one of them and doublechecked to make sure it was secure. Then she motioned for me to climb in.

"We can take turns steering," she decided.

"Okay," I agreed, throwing our bags on to the seat and climbing in after them. She yanked on the reins, and Sorin galloped on the ground with resolution, before taking off towards the sky.

"Thanks for everything, Mr. Koren!" I yelled, waving. Then I wheeled the window shut and slunk into the warm carriage. I spoke through the small window that opened to the outside, where Phoenix sat on a bench, leading Sorin. "How did he agree to a discount? You saved us *eight* liens, and he's the cheapest man I know!"

"There are many things you don't know about me." Phoenix grinned mischievously. Then she leaned in and whispered, "Maybe I know hypnosis." She laughed heartily.

I grinned. "We made out with a steal, didn't we?"

"Yep. It was written all over his face."

# FOUR

**"Wake up." Phoenix leaned** over me. I was cuddled in the corner of the carriage with my blanket. Had I been like this all night? I figured I had, since bags hung under Phoenix's eyes.

"You should've woken me up," I mumbled, picking myself up, slightly embarrassed.

"I thought I just did." Phoenix leaned back. She was munching on half an orange. The other half had been laid aside for me.

"I meant earlier in the night," I told her, seizing the orange and sucking the juice out of it. "Did you stay up *all* night?"

She shrugged. "You were sleeping so soundly, I didn't really feel like waking you up. Besides, Jade from five hundred feet above is even more gorgeous than when you're actually inside."

"Where are we now?" Juice dribbled down my chin.

"Gilmo." Phoenix bit into her orange. "We're going to have to travel during the day if we want to make it to Silenia tomorrow."

"Perfect," I said. "You can get some sleep, and I'll drive the carriage today. But don't sleep too much. You still want to get some rest during the night."

Phoenix could only nod, because her mouth was full. She swallowed, and then peeled another orange piece. "After Silenia, it's only going to be another day to Leon." She eyed her orange warily, before shrugging and sinking her teeth into it. "Silenia's supposed to be the most attractive city in the world, and I've never been. Can you believe that?"

"Neither have I," I admitted, finishing off the last of my orange. Wiping my chin, I zipped open my bag and took out the map. "Alright. So Silenia, then Leon. But we could go Faren, then Leon—"

"I thought of that," Phoenix concurred. "It's faster and all, but Silenia is supposed to be beautiful. They were going to make it the royal city, but that ended up being Gryphon. If I could, I'd put Gryphon on the route so we could see the royal castle where Queen Reyna, King Charles, Prince Liam, and Princess Victoria live, but that's way off course." She gave me a side glance and confessed, "Personally, I'd choose Silenia over Gryphon any day."

I curled the map up and placed it back in my bag. "So, we're in Gilmo right now?"

"Yeah, didn't I tell you that, like, five seconds ago?" Phoenix remarked. Then she frowned at the orange juice on my chin. I obviously hadn't wiped it all off! "Were you always a slob?"

Ignoring her and wiping the juice off my chin, I examined the map and added, "What do you think of touring the city? I mean, we have a bit of time before we need to get going. We should go out, maybe stock up on a bit more food, get cleaned up, and then head to Silenia?"

"That'd be nice," Phoenix approved.

"I'll find a place," I promised as I stood up and stretched. "We can bring the food back to the carriage to eat. Then it's Silenia."

"I think I'm in more of an eat out mood." She grinned. "Why don't we find a nice place to sit down, eat some *restaurant* food, and enjoy some peace and quiet. What do you think?"

I caught sight of the look on her face, and a bad feeling sprouted inside me. Phoenix was having fun running away. She liked her newfound freedom. Even though I was glad to know she wasn't miserable, I knew that getting too casual would give us a one-way ride back home, whether we wanted it or not. I knew, by now, our parents probably would have hired search party after search party, especially in Gilmo, where I practically grew up.

I groaned. "Please tell me you aren't enjoying this."

Phoenix's expression hardened. "Enjoying what? Running away? What's your problem with that?"

"Nothing… I just don't want you to get too casual. We're probably wanted by now. Our parents had to have noticed we're gone. They probably will pay someone a million liens to get us back." As soon as I said it, I wished I could take it back. I could tell by the look on her face that she was about to remind me of what she had done.

"I ran away for you." Phoenix pointed an accusing finger at me. I scooched back. "I'm not allowed to enjoy the little moments?"

"Of course, you are," I added quickly. "I'm just saying that we should be careful…"

It was too late. The damage had been done. Phoenix whisked away, crossing her arms. She pointed her chin at the sky, oblivious to anything I said. I looked away and wished I had kept my mouth shut.

"Do you still want to come?"

She circled back to me with a frown on her face. "I do. But I don't feel like talking much."

Instantly, I knew that talking to Phoenix right now would earn me a seriously depressing evening. When Phoenix told me things like she wanted to be alone or didn't want to talk, I knew that she was super upset and was like an unsteady rope bridge—the slightest shift of weight would make her snap.

I stepped out of the carriage and shut the door behind me. Phoenix stroked Sorin while muttering something under her breath. I sighed. The day was going to be *fun*.

Outside, it was storming. Usually, I don't mind storms; in fact, I find the rain refreshing. But this storm wasn't the refreshing kind. Dark clouds loomed over Gilmo, causing people to scurry across the streets. Rain slashed down, turning to hail as it spiked against my skin. Every so often, a roll of thunder boomed across the sky, shaking everything and startling my eardrums, followed by another flash of deadly lightning.

My mood plummeted. I was sure if I tried hard enough, I'd find an infelici somewhere. Infelicis are ominous creatures that look like bats and are made of storm clouds. They infamously brought bad luck to people who saw them.

"Maybe I should've thought of an umbrella," Phoenix muttered. I scanned the streets for a source of food and shelter from the storm. I spotted a bakery a way off and gestured for Phoenix to follow me inside. Swinging open the door, we both made our way into the cozy room, heated by a blazing fireplace that sent sparks from its lively flames. As soon as I entered, the mouth-watering aroma of sweet cinnamon buns and warm chocolate chip cookies lingered under my nose.

"How much do you think we can buy?" I wondered, eyeing a lady with a large platter of croissants.

Phoenix frowned at the storm. "I don't think we can take off in this weather. We're going to be stuck here longer than planned." She focused on me. "Any plans on a place to stay?"

"I was thinking we could sleep in the carriage," I mumbled, shifting uncomfortably. "I didn't want to risk us being recognized."

"You really planned this out, didn't you?"

I whirled around. "What's that supposed to mean?"

"Nothing," Phoenix muttered. "I just—"

"What?" I asked, glaring at her.

Phoenix spun on me, her eyes full of anger and sorrow. "I miss my family, alright? I'm homesick. This morning was going to be a special family breakfast. Now I'll never see her again." She focused her eyes on the ground quickly, but before she did, something wet streaked her cheek.

I. Was. The. Worst. Best. Friend. Ever.

"I'm sorry, Phoenix." I sat down at a table, pressing my head into my hands. "I'm sorry I pulled you into this."

Phoenix glanced at me. To my surprise, she had recovered, and sadness didn't linger in her eyes. For the first time, I realized how strong Phoenix was.

"If you want to go back, I wouldn't hold it against you." I promised, nevertheless. "If you leave now, I can spend the night here. I can travel with Sorin." I paused. "I'll be fine."

Phoenix shook her head. "I promised you I'd stay."

"I won't be mad if you break it."

"I will be, though." Phoenix loured at the ground. "I'd be mad at myself for making a promise I couldn't keep. I'd be mad that I had an amazing best friend who needed my help, but I didn't help him. I'd be mad every time I looked out the window, knowing you were out there in the cold while I was cozy back home. Knowing you asked for my help, but I didn't help you."

I didn't say anything for a minute. Finally, I mustered up the courage to say, "Can you keep that promise?"

Phoenix inspected me carefully. "I'll hang on to it like my life depends on it." She grinned. Then she side-eyed the samples. "So…" she whistled. "What would you like to eat?"

A few hours later, we climbed back into the carriage, our stomachs full with sugary chocolate chip cookies and buttery croissants that we ate all day long. Phoenix was soaked from head to toe because we had spent the rest of the day touring the city, but I was dry since I willed the water to steer clear of me and the pack. Phoenix warmed herself up until her clothes and her own pack were free of water and cold before searching the back of the carriage for cushioning for the night.

"Three extra cushions back here," Phoenix called out, dragging them back to the front. "Guess Mr. Koren didn't realize it." I was a little ticked off that Phoenix was turning out to be more resourceful than me. I had slept smushed in a corner without thinking of looking for cushions in the back.

We set them up. Phoenix curled up on the bench, and I stretched as much as I could on the little comfort of the cushion. Our beds were small, squished, and pitiful, not like we were used to. *They are still better than nothing,* I told myself over and over again.

I realized we had spent far too much on food. "We have to be more careful," I warned Phoenix, "or we'll end up stuck somewhere with no money."

I'm not sure she heard me. She was too busy frowning at her bed. "How am I ever going to get any sleep?"

I replied sympathetically, "Come on, Phoenix. We're not going to be able to spend every night with fancy beds like we used to. This is part of being on the run. Sleeping in a really uncomfortable bed."

She glared at me. "I can barely feel the cushions," she retorted.

"Do you have any better ideas?"

It wasn't hard to tell she was thinking of bringing up an inn we could stay at, but decided against it. Instead, she rolled over on her bed, pulling her blanket up to her shoulder. "Goodnight," she said gruffly.

I moved my pack a little out of the way. Then I waited for a bit, listening quietly, and soon enough, soft snores filled the carriage. Sighing, I peered out the carriage window, where stars glistened in the twilight sky, wondering if I had made a huge mistake.

"Goodnight," I whispered. Then I closed my eyes.

***

It felt like I'd just sunken into a desirable sleep when I heard Phoenix caterwauling my name blaringly: "Seamus! *Seamus*!"

I sat up groggily and rubbed my eyes. "What?" I grumbled, thinking Phoenix had woken me up because she couldn't sleep. "Go back to sleep, Phoenix. You need the rest." But when I switched my gaze to the seat, Phoenix wasn't there. Panicking, I sprang up, banging my head on the roof of the carriage. Moaning, I turned around woozily. Phoenix was tapping her foot on the ground with the door of the carriage open. Sunlight shone on to her hair. I groaned.

"Is it morning already?" I rolled over, trying to get comfortable again.

Phoenix nudged me, and ignoring my complaints, she said, "I've got news for you, sleepyhead. When you're on the run, you have to wake up early when no one's out and about. Hurry up!"

Jeez.

*Someone* woke up too cheery this morning.

"You better hurry up, Seamus. We want to get to Selina before we get old," she teased, patting the back of the carriage. "Also, your turn to steer."

"Oh, yeah," I remembered, and stood up.

I clambered out of the back and pulled myself onto the bench in the front. Sorin whinnied happily towards me. He was munching on a large carrot, and his mouth was wet with water.

I flicked the reins. "Okay, Sorin, listen. I've rode a pegasus before—her name is River—but I've never driven a carriage, so you're going to have to work with me here, alright?"

Sorin neighed in understanding.

"Thanks, boy," I reached out to stroke his neck. Then I flicked the reins again. "Let's go! Take off!"

Okay, I needed to work on my pegasus talk. But in my defense, I was used to riding *on* the horse, not on the bench of a carriage tied *to* the horse. Usually, all I had to do to get River to take off was click my heels gently against her side, and we'd go spinning into the sky.

Fortunately, Sorin understood, and he spread his wings as I braced myself for impact, spiraling towards the sky. I squinted at the ground, torn between fear and marvel as I watched the people shopping on the streets grow smaller and smaller.

"Wow," I murmured.

The sun hung just above us, its rays streaming through the clouds down upon Gilmo. It was the perfect day for flying with River. I felt a tug at my stomach, and I tried not to think about my beloved pegasus.

"How far is Silenia from Gilmo?" I shouted to Phoenix.

"About three hours. Once we get there, we can eat the food we brought for lunch. How are you doing up there? Not scared, right?"

"Nope. It's fantastic!" I stole a peek over my shoulder at Phoenix, who watched me with her head out the window. "I love it up here. This is way different from jumping off a cliff, even if it is into the ocean."

"Just get ready for a long ride," she warned and stuck her head back into the carriage. I squinted through the sharp wind, beginning to wish I had brought gloves. The cold snapped at me relentlessly, and the only thing I wore was my thin hoodie and pants.

Not to mention, it wasn't easy keeping my eyes from straying to the ground. As soon as I glanced down, buildings as small as ants and tiny little candles illuminating them sparkled below me.

*If I trip myself, or lay down to go to sleep, or fall asleep at all…*

Shivering at the thought, I nervously scooted closer to the middle, trying not to think about how far down the ground was. I marveled at how different flying on a horse felt compared to on a carriage bench attached to one. Sorin neighed reassuringly.

"Thanks, Sorin, but you just keep your eyes on the road—or, uh, the sky. We don't want to crash."

Sorin whinnied softly. I wasn't surprised. Pegasi took the place of the most intelligent animal in the world. Not as smart as Armanians, of course, or we wouldn't be the dominant race, but pretty close. Pegasi know what you're feeling, broadly understand what you're saying, and always try to make you feel better.

I focused on the sky ahead of me and felt myself relax. The wind stopped cutting through my skin, and though the cold numbed my fingers, there was something refreshing about it. Even glancing down to see the sparkling city wasn't all that bad.

"Just keep going north!" Phoenix shouted behind me.

"No problem!" I yelled, grinning. "Get ready for Silenia!"

\*\*\*

The first impression that Silenia struck on me was: *Big.*

I am not kidding. The first thing that came to my mind when Sorin softly landed us in an out-of-the-way alley was, *Boy, this place is huge.* It was surprising Silenia wasn't the royal city. And how had I never visited? My parents promised me we'd visit all the best cities, and who could describe Silenia as anything short of the best?

Even in the small alley we landed in, the grand architecture of Silenia loomed over us proudly. Huge buildings made of colored glass, with large windows depicting mythical creatures and heroes of Timnock, stood on the streets. Grand cathedrals rose far above the rest of the buildings. In the distance, I could make out rolling hills with the large flag of Timnock waving proudly in the air.

"You were right, Phoenix," I admitted as I took in the breathtaking sight. "Silenia is worth stopping for."

Phoenix gave me a smug grin. "You should always listen to me."

I rolled my eyes. "Whatever."

Phoenix stroked Sorin's soft mane. "Let's take Sorin with us to tour the city and find a place to store the carriage," she said.

"Good idea. Let's also find a place to buy a map of Silenia," I added.

A map would definitely be cheaper than a tour guide. And besides, the news of two runaway kids was probably widespread now, and a tour guide was more likely to identify us than a map.

"Come on. Let's grab our packs and get going. Silenia's huge, and it's not going to tour itself."

Phoenix smirked as she climbed into the carriage. She slung her pack over her shoulder. Then she climbed out and strode to Sorin, trying to unlatch him from the carriage. "Stay still, Sorin," Phoenix complained as Sorin shifted uncomfortably.

It took a while, but she finally got Sorin free. Sorin flapped his wings, stretching, knocking Phoenix to the ground. She landed on her bottom in a huge puddle, splashing water everywhere and splattering mud all over her clothes. Phoenix groaned.

"Sorin... *seriously?*"

"Aw, give the pegasus a break. He's been latched on to that thing for days without rest. I should've realized he was itching to get out." I strode to him, barely noticing Phoenix holding out a hand, waiting to be lifted off the ground. Instead, I stroked Sorin. "Sorry," I muttered.

"Gee, thanks," Phoenix grumbled, picking herself off the ground. "Thanks for asking me if I broke anything after I nearly broke something."

"What?" I asked distractedly. I turned around to find Phoenix caked with dirt. Her golden-brown hair was mussed up and her clothes and legs were covered with mud. "Ugh. After we tour Silenia, I don't care if we're on the run or not, we need to get you a shower. Right now, we should find that map. Silenia has got to be much more beautiful than what we see from this spot. Come on! What are you waiting for?"

Phoenix shrugged. "Let's go."

\*\*\*

"Do I know you?"

The man at the counter of a souvenir shop was staring down at us. His eyes were big, and when he widened them, it seemed they were out of place and a bit scary. *This man might know us from the news,* I realized. I shifted nervously and chanced a glance at Phoenix for help, who hadn't lost her stoical expression.

"We're stunt extras for movies," Phoenix responded smoothly before I could say something stupid. "We've been in a few of them."

The man didn't look convinced, but he shrugged it off. "My name is Jason. Welcome to Silenia." The way he said it, he might as well have been welcoming us to Freian, the dark side of the underworld, for people who had done more bad than good. "There are plenty of things to do in this wondrous city. Would you like a map?"

"Um... sure." I frowned, wondering how someone could make the things he said sound so depressing. "We'll take one."

"Great." Jason stared at us blankly. "Would you mind me asking for a jin? That's how much it costs."

"No problem," Phoenix complied, reaching into her pack and pulling out a jin. She handed it to Jason, who snatched it out of her hands so quickly, Phoenix jumped and recoiled her hand like a whip.

"Is this real?" he asked. Before either of us could answer, he opened his mouth and chomped on it. Before

I could ask him if he ate breakfast or not, and explain that when people said they wanted money for breakfast, it was not to literally *eat* the money, he placed it inside a drawer, concluding that the coin was genuine.

"Uh…" Phoenix looked like she was trying to hold in a hacking cough.

Jason stepped towards the shelves on his right and flipped through the papers that were stacked on top of a shelf. He pulled out a small, folded piece of paper and placed it on the table. When neither of us moved, he pushed it towards us.

"The map," he explained.

"Um, yeah." Phoenix reached over and used her fingertip to edge the map back, as if afraid that he had bitten on the map to make sure that was real as well. "Thanks."

"No problem." Jason flashed us a smile that was very clearly forced. "The door's that way." He pointed to the door we had entered from.

I nodded, mumbled a thanks, and dragged Phoenix outside the shop. Sorin was grazing in a patch of grass outside and neighed cheerily when we returned. We exchanged disgusted looks, and I muttered, "Do you reckon the guy ate breakfast? Maybe he was tasting it."

For a minute, we were both silent, and then we burst out laughing. We laughed until our stomachs hurt. I sucked in a breath, trying to calm myself, because if I laughed anymore, I'd pass out from lack of air.

"Anyway," I managed, wheezing and clutching my stomach, "where do you want to go first?"

"The Saint Amethyst Cathedral, most definitely," Phoenix replied, recovering from the hysterical fit of laughter as she unfolded the map gingerly. "It's supposed to be magical. All my friends recommended it. It's never crowded, because they only let so many people in at a time. It's supposed to be very peaceful."

"Doesn't that mean longer lines?"

Phoenix shot me a deadly look. "This is a once-in-a-lifetime chance, and you're worried about *long lines*? Come on! This is why everyone comes to Silenia. We'd be morons if we missed it."

"I'm a moron," I said, snatching the map from her and flipping through it. "We're skipping."

"You aren't serious."

"Dead serious. Hmmm, Sorin looks hungry. We'll have to stop to feed him along the way," I decided, then I peeked back at her. "Come on. Let's go tour the rest of Silenia. If that place is so famous, there's going to be long lines that probably go down the street. We're going to miss out on the rest of Silenia if we wait so long."

Phoenix rolled her eyes. "What's the rush?" Before I could explain that we were wanted across Timnock, she cut in, "Seamus, I ran away from my entire life for you, and you can't wait a bit to get to Leon?"

Oh, great.

We were going to that cathedral, whether I liked it or not.

\*\*\*

It was ten o'clock in the morning. Phoenix led Sorin, who looked very uncomfortable walking on the stones of the street, and I followed from the side. I would've followed from behind, but I've worked enough with pegasi to know that being as far away as you can from the back is always best.

Clouds filled the sky, looming over the streets. Not the best day for touring, but it was impossible to talk Phoenix out of it. Just looking at her face, you could tell she was determined to get to the cathedral, with or without me.

Phoenix scrutinized the map. "The cathedral is near the east end of the town. The streets there are more peaceful. I guess that's why they put it there."

"That's not too bad," I admitted. "The east end of town isn't very far from here. We could make it and tour the cathedral before lunch, and we'd have the rest of the day to tour the *rest* of Silenia." I shot Phoenix a look. "I can't believe we're losing half our day just to see some stupid cathedral."

"It's not *some stupid cathedral.*" Phoenix wagged her finger at me. "It's the Saint Amethyst Cathedral, and it's *famous*. Honestly, I'm surprised you've never heard of it. Nearly everyone at school's been to it, and nearly everyone at school says it's the best one. There's no way I'm letting you drag me along a tour while knowing I'm going to miss one of the reasons Silenia is famous."

I shrugged. Personally, I wasn't a big fan of cathedrals, and I thought the rest of Silenia would be way cooler, but when I looked at Phoenix, I knew there was no way I could say no. She was right. She *had* run away from everything she knew for me. So why couldn't I do this for her?

"Alright," I huffed. "How far east is it?"

"Not that far," Phoenix promised, squinting back down at the map. "It's just a little way over there. Follow me." Then she tucked the map back in her pocket, took hold of Sorin's lead, and began walking, leaving me to follow.

Going to the east end of town didn't take nearly as long as I thought it would. The walk there wasn't all that bad, either. We passed large buildings that lit up and bakeries with delectable smells emanating out the door. Libraries that stood up to thirty floors high towered over us, and we passed the Garden of Amezula, a huge garden with nearly every kind of flower in Arma. We even came across roadside performers once and stopped to watch the show and get free popcorn.

"Bleh." Phoenix made a face and threw the popcorn aside. "No wonder it was free. Way too much salt and butter."

I had given up eating the popcorn a while ago. "How much farther until we get to Saint Amethyst?"

Phoenix unfurled the map. "Not much longer. The cathedral is just half a mile away. It shouldn't take very long to walk."

"Do you think— " I stopped. Phoenix let out a small gasp, and her face went white. Her eyes widened, and she pointed at something behind me, her face petrified.

"What?" I asked, wondering if this was one of her tricks.

When she didn't answer, I rolled my eyes and turned around, but when my eyes fell on the sight that awaited me, my heart almost stopped.

A large, burly man glared down at me. He had crooked, yellow teeth and was completely bald. Despite having no hair whatsoever on his head, he still sported a large beard that almost dangled from his chin. Scars cut through and deepened his uneven face, and there was one intimidating, round, glass eye where his normal eye was supposed to be.

Though he was pretty scary looking himself, and I probably would've run either way, the scary part was this: the guy was holding a knife.

The knife was at least a couple of feet long—way too big to be legal to carry around. It definitely wasn't legal to take with you while creepily stalking some random kids.

I gulped, watching his one eye move from me to Phoenix. His glass eye didn't move at all.

"Um, excuse me, sir. Are we in your way?"

"Yes," he answered in a deep, scratchy voice.

I moved to the side.

He didn't lower the knife.

Sorin neighed nervously.

"Do you need something?" I asked skittishly. "Because if you don't, we'll just, um, be on our way— "

"No leaving," the man ordered roughly, stepping in front of me.

I turned around to look at Phoenix and mouthed, *"Help."*

I shouldn't have turned around.

The man grabbed me, wrapping his arm around my neck. I struggled against him, clawing at his hands. Phoenix's eyes went wide with shock, and she seized her pack. He stuffed a cloth in my mouth, causing everything to muddle and blur until they were fuzzy. I barely remember Phoenix screaming, "SEAMUS!" before the man muffled her shouts and Sorin galloped down the street.

Then everything went black.

# FIVE

**When my eyes first opened,** pitch black surrounded me, and a ringing noise echoed in my ears. I was barely aware of the chains that held my hands behind my chair. Then I blinked again, and a fuzzy sense of my surroundings came to me.

*What happened? Where am I? Who took us? Why did they take us?*

That's when I really woke up. I blinked hard and shook my head, the ringing sound disappearing. Glancing up, I realized I was in a large, circular cell. The only thing to look at was the cold stones that made up the wall and a rectangular cut out that I assumed was a door. Then a terrifying thought hit me:

*Where's Phoenix?*

I whipped my head around the room, but the same sight greeted me everywhere I looked: bare stone walls.

The panic inside me grew by the second.

*What did they do to Phoenix?*

Footsteps stomped up the stairs and towards me. I desperately tried to twist my hands out of the chains and regain clarity in my head. The next question hit me:

*How am I going to escape?*

A loud bang made me jump. Someone cursed outside the door and someone else shouted.

"Open this door!" commanded a low voice. The voice was too high-pitched to be that of the man who had taken me. With a great amount of scraping and pushing, the door swung open, screeching against the ground with an ear-splitting sound.

The first person that strode in was a woman with an evil-looking Belgian Shepherd trailing behind her. The malicious glare that stood on her face told me crossing her would be a really bad idea. Her violet eyes were sharp and clear, and her flowing black hair reached past her waist. She wore a black dress with full sleeves, and the hem of her dress swept the floor and spiked upwards.

Behind the Shepherd was a scrawny looking fellow. He had shaggy hair and looked like he had tried to grow a beard, but had failed miserably. Holes decorated his clothes. His vest hung on his shoulders, and his shaggy pants looked like he'd got them from a dumpster.

The woman eyed me with a cryptic look that seemed like a mix of distaste and delight. I tried to focus on her, but her eyes were extremely distracting.

The pounding of my heart thumped in my ears.

*Will I make it out of here alive?*

"If it isn't our little hero," the woman hissed, stepping closer to me. I coiled back. "I've been wanting to meet you, Seamus."

A thousand questions danced on the tip of my tongue, but the only important one remained sharp and clear in my mind. "What did you do with Phoenix?"

The woman's face changed to an expression of revulsion that I resented. "Phoenix? That girl you were traveling with? Well, if we're being honest here, she was a handful. The girl is not only fiery, but she also literally has the power over fire, as she demonstrated for us earlier."

Pure hatred and enmity swelled inside me. I was going to hurt this evil woman.

To my own delight, I noticed nasty burns on her skin, stretching up and down her arms. *That's Phoenix alright.*

"She put up quite a fight, and I'm sure she has potential. But I have no use for the girl, except maybe dinner for my babies." The woman smiled wickedly.

"Y-your *babies*?" I stuttered.

"Oh, yes. They've been hungry for *so* long. The meat I've been giving them hasn't been nearly enough, and they need their strength for the battle." The woman licked her lips. "They'll be ever so pleased."

I stared at her, trying to steady my thumping heart and racing breath. "Who are you? Why have you kidnapped us?"

"I only wanted to kidnap *you*, but the girl got in the way. And Master hates loose ends." The woman cackled. "No worries. She'll come of use to us tonight."

The horrible words gutted me like a sword.

*Keep her talking,* I thought nervously, trying to ignore the stabbing panic inside me. *The more she talks, the longer I have to think. The longer I have to get Phoenix out of here alive.*

"Who are you?" I asked. "Where am I?"

"I couldn't very well tell you where you are, now can I?" She came closer to me so that her violet eyes were inches away from my face. "How could I give away my little secret?" She laughed maniacally. "As for your other question, hero, my name is Calypso."

"Why did you take us? Are you part of the police?"

As soon as I said it, I realized how stupid it sounded. No, police didn't send creeps to stalk kids with an illegal knife. They didn't kidnap runaways and chain them to a chair in an unknown location to interrogate them.

Was this an interrogation?

I still didn't know.

"*The police*?" Calypso cried out in disdain. "No, boy, I'm not part of the police! I'm part of something far greater!"

"What?" I asked, my mind racing to find an escape.

"I'm part of a *plan*. A masterplan to defeat Arma, to take it over. It has been forming for years. We've carefully built it, bit by bit. Arma is too strong to take head on. So, we came up with a *plan* to weaken it. We came up with a *plan* to steal what makes Arma powerful. Once we've done that, we'll be able to take it over and rid it of the useless royals! Ah, but don't worry. You'll be on the winning side when that happens."

Silence.

*What?*

No… no… *no…*

*This isn't real!* A panicked scream inside me screeched. *I'm dreaming! I'm going to wake up in my own bed this morning, my parents won't be divorced, and I won't be chained to a chair!*

Even as I thought it, I knew it wasn't true.

"You want me to *join* you?" I breathed softly.

"Yes," A thin smile curled across Calypso's lips. "I want you to join the winning side."

"You're crazy!" I yelled, struggling against the chains restlessly and twisting my body. "I'm never joining you!"

"And there's the catch," Calypso grinned. "If you don't agree to come to the *winning* side, then we're going to have to kill you."

Anger and fear boomed inside me.

"Can't you just let me go?" I squeaked.

"*No,*" she thundered. "You either help us win or die."

"No... I—I *won't*—"

Calypso cackled like my fear amused her. "You see, Master has ordered me to recruit you to our side. If you don't agree, we kill you. So that's what's going to happen?"

"*Master?*" I croaked, trying to remember the need to stall.

There wouldn't be any point in stalling if I wasn't alive to carry out my escape plan. *Except... I don't have a plan.* I told myself to shut up and think positive.

"None of your business," Calypso snapped. "What *is* your business is the deal I just offered you." Then she leaned in and whispered, "I'm warning you—your death will be very painful."

As she pulled away, I let out a shaky breath. Still, I tried to steady my voice as I asked, "Why do you want me so badly?"

"Oh, it would avoid a *lot* of bloodshed, and I'm not really in the mood for killing." She shrugged like *I'm not really in the mood for killing* was something people just went around saying. "But trust me, if I have to kill, I will. I'm on strict orders from my master."

Strict orders from her master?

No.

*No!*

I needed to get Phoenix out alive.

What choice did I have?

"Fine," I whispered, my knees shaking and my fingers white and trembling. "I'll join. On one condition."

"We don't take conditions," the lanky man snarled.

Calypso whipped around. "Shut up, Scrawny." She turned back to me. "Spit."

"Phoenix gets to live. You let her go."

"But she's a free meal!" Calypso protested in a whiny voice. "She should at least be kept as a slave. Maybe that'll teach the nasty girl a lesson. Then maybe she'll think twice before burning Calypso!"

I took a deep breath, attempting to clear the fear and panic from my head. "What would your master say if you could've had me on your side, but you turned it down for petty revenge?"

Calypso looked stricken. *Score!* I had painted her in a corner. She mumbled, whined, growled but eventually acceded.

"Fine," Calypso agreed, disgruntled. "The girl is released, but in return you will serve in my army."

I nearly choked on my own spit. "Your *army?*"

"Yes." Calypso nodded as if it made perfect sense. "You will join my army, and in turn we will release Phoenix."

"But, my mistress…" Scrawny watched Calypso from the back of the room, right next to the door. "How can you be sure that this boy is the one? The prophecy only mentions—"

"*Shut up, you fool!*" Calypso gave Scrawny such a stern look that Scrawny stepped back and shuddered.

Scrawny swallowed and nodded. Then he flashed me a piercing glare, his expression clearly conveying his hatred for me.

Calypso took a breath, attempting to calm herself. Then she flashed her eyes at me. "Scrawny, get me my knife."

"Wait, what? I thought we had a deal!"

"Just because I can't kill you, doesn't mean I can't play with you a bit. A few cuts and bruises will be good for you. It'll make you understand who's boss. Besides, doing it as your friend witnesses my craftsmanship will be double fun. She'll be able to watch you get some of the worst scars imaginable. *Guards*!" Scrawny's face lit up for the first time. The way he licked his lips, it was clear he relished the idea.

Three guards marched into the room through the open door. They all wore grey uniforms and an odd symbol on their shirts—it looked like the shadow of the

Bridge. Thick, black masks covered their faces with thin holes around their eyes. One of them unleashed a knife from his belt and charged towards me threateningly.

"NO! Leave me alone!" I screamed.

I squeezed my eyes shut, preparing myself for harrowing pain, but all that happened was the guard seizing the chain. As soon as his fingertips touched the metal, the chains melted to bubbly goo on the floor.

Horrified, I sprang up, ready to freeze this guy and shatter him to pieces, but before I could make a move, he snatched my arms and forced me into the chains he had ready. Then he held me tightly so I couldn't move. No matter how much I squirmed and struggled against him, his firm hold on me didn't loosen.

"No! That's not fair!" I screamed. "Let me go! *Let me go!*"

Calypso, who stood in the corner while stroking her shepherd, rolled her violet eyes. "Take him out. I think it's high time he learned how to talk to his new mistress."

*"No! Let me go! Let me go!"*

The guard forced me out of the room, past Calypso, who was examining her blood-red nails, and Scrawny, who glared threateningly at me. The guards led me down a spiraling staircase and through a long, stone hall. With each step, I knew I was getting closer and closer towards my own room of torture. They forced me down long hallways, but not the slightest thing changed. Everything was cold, unwelcoming, and made of stone.

My stomach turned as we walked farther down into the maze of halls.

How many others were forced into labor by Calypso? How many others were tortured? Killed?

How many more like me?

*Don't think like that,* I told myself as I reminded my lungs that they needed air. *This is going to be okay. This is going to be okay. This is going to be okay.*

I repeated that to myself several times, but I couldn't make myself believe it.

After passing countless doors and turning into another mundane hall, the guards led me into a room.

The room didn't help the slightest.

The first thing I noticed were the bright windows on the side. This gave me little comfort, because when I squinted through the dirty glass, all I could see was the greenery of a forest, and there weren't any forests anywhere near Silenia or anyplace I wanted to be.

It got much worse.

When I turned my focus away from the windows, I froze while trying to remember to breathe. In front of me was a small, wooden chair that was nailed to the floor. That was pretty creepy itself, but the worst part about it were the chains that hung from the seat and crept down to the floor.

"Move it," a guard grunted, pushing me forward. Stumbling and nearly falling over, I was forced into the room and into the chair. The guard snatched the chain while using only one hand to hold me down, but his one hand was more than enough. Every guard was burly and had muscles so big it was a surprise they didn't rip through their uniforms.

Even though my hopes were dying, and I knew there was almost no chance of escape, I flailed and kicked at the guard furiously.

"Let me *go!*" I shouted, distress fighting in my eyes.

The guard ignored my racket.

It didn't take long to get me secured in the chains. Once he finished, the guard turned to face the other guards.

"Get the girl," he muttered menacingly. "I'll watch the boy."

"You all could go. I'm chained down now," I tried weakly, willing my hands not to tremble.

The guard didn't answer.

Breathe. *Breathe.*

How was I going to get out? If I stayed, I'd look like the guy who kidnapped us—deformed with missing parts on me. My eyes widened as I realized *why* the guy looked like he did.

Trying not to think about that, I searched desperately for another way out. There were windows, and judging by the scenery outside, we weren't that far off the ground. We could jump and make a run for it. But did the windows even open? What if they didn't? And how was I going to get out of my chains? Phoenix didn't have any weapons or sharp things at all. Neither did I. Could I break it with my own strength? Maybe I could use my abilities and freeze it off? Only if I could move my arms to work the magic spell. Phoenix could burn the chains, but she'd be held by a guard. If she managed to burn the guard holding her, a big enough burn to get him to let go of her, she might be able to break my chains. But what about the guy with the knife? He'd slash her for sure. Maybe she could avoid it. Maybe she could set fire to the entire place and come to my aid. But couldn't that kill us as well? That'd also block off the door. If the windows didn't open, we'd be dead.

There were about a million things that could go wrong with my plans, and most of them included getting us killed. Was taking that risk worth it? Would Phoenix even leave me when she got the chance to leave? This was getting worse and worse.

One thing still remained that I could try now, and considering the situation, anything was worth a shot.

I closed my eyes and focused on the water particles in the air. I gathered them to where my chains were. How long would it take to freeze them off?

*That doesn't matter.* I told myself. *Focus.*

I concentrated harder than I'd ever concentrated before and waited for the chains to grow cold, but they never did. My eyes flew open. Why wasn't my ability working?

That's when it hit me.

In school, we studied magical artifacts. They taught us about how, in prisons, they used special chains to block magical abilities and avoid criminals escaping.

These chains weren't regular chains. They were magical chains that blocked my power!

That's it. We. Were. Doomed.

Two guards came back with Phoenix squeezed between them. My voice caught in my throat when I saw her. She was blindfolded and had many nasty bruises running up and down her arms. Rage rampaged through me. *When I get my hands on Calypso...*

The guard ripped off her blindfold. Phoenix watched me with her eyes wide with fear and panic. She mouthed, *No powers.*

I nodded. What were we supposed to do?

"The knife?" One of the guards held out his hand to the other guard. Obediently, he was handed a similar knife that the man who kidnapped us had been holding. I squeezed my eyes shut. This was it. I was going to experience unimaginable pain.

"NO!" Phoenix screamed, struggling and kicking with all her might. The guard kicked her to the floor, making her grunt with pain.

"Stop it!" I screamed, trying to stand up. "Let her go! You said you'd let her go!"

The guards paid no attention to me. They paid more attention to the large knife they were now sharpening.

Uh-oh.

Suddenly, a large *BOOM* thundered upstairs followed by loud shouts. The guards squinted up, shocked. Little stone pieces rained down from the ceiling. It sounded like someone had lit fireworks inside.

"Go see what's happening," the guard with the knife ordered. "I'm going to stay here and make sure the job gets done."

The other guards nodded, chained Phoenix, threw open the door, and marched out of the room in a single file. When they left, I turned back to the guard. A thousand things went through my head as the sound of the knife sharpening echoed in my ears.

Why even bother?

There was no way to escape. There was no magic. I didn't have any weapons. Even if Phoenix somehow managed to help me, we couldn't take the guard down with nothing but our bare hands and no magic. The guy looked like he did two hundred pushups a day along with seven hundred squats.

*BOOM!* This one shook the room. I gripped the chair so tightly my knuckles turned white. Phoenix shrunk into the shadows and looked at me with wide eyes.

It sounded like someone had let off a cannon. The guard looked at the ceiling as a few small shards of stone rained down for a moment, but then turned back to his knife like it was no big deal. I glanced at Phoenix, who was frowning at the ceiling.

"We need to get out of here," I hissed so quietly, I was unsure if I had even said it. But Phoenix gazed at me and nodded in understanding. Then she tilted her head at the windows and mouthed, *Escape.* But I burst her bubble when I held up my chains and tilted my head towards the guard and his knife.

Phoenix shook her head. "We have to try," she hissed fiercely.

I studied the determined expression on her face for a moment and a ruthless, burning fire sparked inside of me.

*We have to try.*

Phoenix held up three of her fingers. *Three... Two... One!*

I seized the bottom of the wooden chair and pulled as hard as I could. To my surprise, it came out on my second pull. I kicked it across the room with my hands still chained behind my back and darted to the window, Phoenix following behind me.

"HEY!" the guard shouted, whirling around with the knife sharpener swinging in his hand.

Phoenix raised a foot and kicked open the window. It flung open, the force of the blow so great that the glass shattered to pieces. I glanced down, but my heart almost stopped when I realized it was a thirty-foot drop.

*I'm not afraid of heights. I'm not afraid of heights.*

The guard lunged at me, but Phoenix whirled around and kicked his stomach furiously. He lost his balance and fell backwards, but his knife grazed my leg as he fell. Pain exploded in my leg as I gasped. Phoenix grabbed my hand. We studied each other for a moment and exchanged a silent conversation.

Both of us, with our hands still chained behind our backs, crouched down, ready to hurtle out the window and plunge to the ground in escape, when the door banged open, and four men with blue robes and badges reading *MAD* came bursting through the door.

MAD?

By this time, the guard had recovered from his blow, and he steadied his knife as he slowly approached us, like we were unstable wild animals. Then one of the men, entirely unfazed, pulled out a wand slickly and shot a beam of green light at the guard. The guard's face, which was scarlet with anger, went rigid and still. His entire body froze, and he tipped over backwards, landing in a crumpled heap on the floor.

Phoenix stared down at the guard and then gazed at the man.

"You're a wizard," she gasped.

"And I can tell you're very smart," the wizard said, hastily rushing over. By the way he said it, I couldn't tell if he was being sarcastic or not. He pointed his wand at Phoenix's chains and fired a beam of blue light at it. "Snap the chain," he directed.

"How—"

"Just do it!"

Glaring, Phoenix pulled her hands apart and snapped the chain behind her back. She widened her eyes when the chain fell apart and the cuffs broke against each other. She gaped at the wizard in awe.

The wizard turned and raised an eyebrow at me. Obedient to his silent order, I held out my chains and watched in amazement as a beam of blue light shot from his wands and on to the chains. I snapped them as easily as if they were hardened clay and tossed them on the ground.

Turning my attention away from the broken chains, I frowned at the wizard.

"Who are you?" I asked suspiciously.

"No time to explain! Amaranth, guard the door while I get these two out. Everyone else, come with me!" the wizard ordered.

Amaranth defended the door with his wand ready while the other wizards crowded around us, all squinting down the window. One of them reached into his pocket and unveiled a bottle. He muttered something under his breath and dropped it out the window.

My eyes narrowed. What were they doing?

More importantly, were they here to help or hurt?

They had just saved me from imminent torture. Hopefully, that wasn't because they wanted to imprison and torture me for the same reasons Calypso did. Even worse, they might not cut a deal with me for Phoenix.

"Everyone, stay close!" the wizard yelled. The other wizards stretched their legs and jumped out the window. Listening closely, I heard the low thump of their smooth landing when they hit the ground.

"Hey!" someone shouted from below. I peered over the edge to find smoke engulfing most of the guards, and barely visible red lights streaking across the smoke. For a minute, they all stopped, and then someone from below shouted, "Clear!"

"HEY!" A familiar but unwelcome voice bellowed from the door. I whirled around to find Amaranth shooting spells at Calypso, who came with an army of canines. Dogs, wolves, foxes, and jackals lunged at

Amaranth. He barely kept up with all of them now, and I didn't see how it was possible that he could manage to last much longer.

Fear pumped inside me as I stood, frozen, watching Calypso's furious canines destroy Amaranth—the man who had saved our lives.

"Go! *Jump*!" The wizard who had helped us snap our chains shook me, pointing out the window.

Phoenix looked stricken. "But, the wizard back there— Amaranth—"

"He's a very talented wizard, but the mission is to get both of you back to headquarters safely. So *jump* now unless you want to be dinner for Calypso's wolves!"

Phoenix touched my arm, and we exchanged a look. She seemed to know what I was thinking because she whispered, "Together."

*I'm not afraid of heights. I'm not afraid of heights.*

Summoning all the courage inside me, I grasped Phoenix tightly, sucked in a deep breath, and hurtled over the edge.

# SIX

**Pain.**

*Excruciating* pain.

Despite being cushioned by the forcefield of magic set by the wizards, my leg throbbed, stinging my senses and forcing me to grab on to Phoenix in order to remain standing. The world shook as soon as I landed, and my wound screamed, ready to give away, but before I could fall, Phoenix steadied me and inspected my leg closely.

I bit my lip in an effort not to shout out. My hands curled into fists, and my nails dug into my palms.

The ground was fuzzy around me, but I forced myself to look up. The smoke cleared to show the result of the struggle. Five guards lay unconscious on the ground.

Despite the suffering they'd caused, I hoped they weren't dead.

"We need to move," The words on my lips were hoarse and I was finding it difficult to focus. "We—" I wheezed, trying to ignore the tormenting cut. "We have to get out of here. Before *she* comes back." Dread coursed through me at the thought of Calypso.

"We aren't going anywhere until I've seen your cut," Phoenix warned furiously. "This is *my* fault. If we'd just waited instead of trying to escape—"

"It's fine," I promised, forcing a smile on to my face. It didn't look like Phoenix was convinced—in fact, she looked even more worried, so I stopped and changed track. "It only started hurting a bit when we landed. It doesn't hurt that much."

"Stay still," Phoenix commanded, crouching down.

Knowing there was no way to show Phoenix I was fine (she could detect fake almost as well as she could fake), I glanced up and squinted at the window, searching for a sign that the wizards who were left behind when we jumped, including Amaranth, had gotten away. Red flashes appeared and disappeared as fast as they came.

"OVER HERE!" someone yelled out. Reluctantly, I turned away from the window and scanned the smoke for a source of the voice. Two wizards waved their arms wildly at me. They stood next to a chariot with two pegasi latched on. In fact, one of those looked familiar…

*"Sorin?"* Phoenix gasped with disbelief, breaking away from concentrating on my wound. "But, how—?"

"I don't know, but we better get going!" I warned. Phoenix, understanding we had no choice, ducked under my arm and held me up, supporting me so that it would be easier to walk. I limped towards the carriage, my arm around her as I balanced my weight. Even with the support, every time my leg hit the ground, the gash throbbed. I squeezed my eyes shut and tried to ignore the crucifying pain.

"Get in," one of the wizards ordered as he climbed into the driver's seat. The other wizard was already inside.

Phoenix helped me inside and climbed in after me, but when she got in, she didn't shut the door behind her.

"What about the other two wizards? They're still up there!"

"She's right," I managed. By the way both of them looked at me, the expression on my face didn't agree with my statement.

The driver shook his head. "They have another way of getting back. Right now, the only important thing is getting you back to headquarters safely. So, close the door!"

Phoenix hesitated.

"They'll make it back! Trust me! Shut it!"

Still hesitant, but with no other choice, Phoenix slammed it close, and the driver flicked the reins. The pegasi took off, stampeding on the ground before taking flight into the sky. I heaved a huge breath, trying to comprehend what had just happened and why, while attempting to ignore the pain. Never, in a million years, would I have thought I'd do any of the things I just did.

"You okay?" Phoenix asked, a concerned look on her face. She touched my arm. "You've got goosebumps all over, and you're shaking."

"Am I?" I asked weakly. "I guess that's what happens after such a lovely evening."

Then Phoenix did something completely unexpected—she wrapped her arms around me and hugged me. It was over as soon as it started, but I stared at her, wondering if she was the real Phoenix. Not once in my entire life had Phoenix hugged me, because she wasn't that kind of person. Pheonix + sarcasm? Yes! Phoenix + emotional expression? NO! My eyes became moist, not because of the pain but the heartwarming love of my best friend.

I stared out the window, my cheeks slightly red. The place we were imprisoned in looked like a fortress, and it felt good to leave it behind. More than that—it felt *safe*. A safety that I had secretly longed for ever since leaving the comfort of home.

Then I remembered Calypso's plans.

Oh, brother.

I really didn't want to talk about Calypso—*ever*—but I knew what she told me couldn't wait.

"Excuse me, sir." I tapped the savior wizard sitting next to me.

The man turned to me, his kind blue eyes immediately noticeable. "My name is Glavio. You can call me that."

"Er… Glavio, when Calypso questioned me, she mentioned a few things that were disturbing."

"Disturbing?" Glavio's expression instantly became serious.

"She said she was trying to weaken Arma, bit by bit, until we aren't as powerful as we are now. Her goal is the conquest of Arma. Her assistant also let it slip that he wasn't sure if I was 'the one.' He also said something about 'the other one'? Do you have any idea what that could mean?"

Glavio's eyebrows creased, causing lines to etch in his forehead.

"Her assistant said he wasn't sure if you were the one?"

I nodded, a feeling of foreboding sinking within my stomach.

"What could that possibly mean?" Phoenix frowned.

I watched Glavio's face, and when he said, "I have no idea," I knew he was lying. There are people who are good at lying, and people who just can't. Glavio was the second kind. But he *did* save our lives, so I decided to drop the subject.

Phoenix's eyes narrowed, but she, like me, was probably too exhausted to interrogate him. Instead, she asked, "How did you find Sorin?"

"Sorin?" Glavio asked blankly. Realization dawned on his features as he asked, "You mean that small pegasus up there? Oh, well, we found him where you were kidnapped. He was quite distressed. We knew one of Calypso's men was sent there, but after he took you, he vanished. It was lucky we managed to track you down before they did any real damage." He gazed at my leg long enough to make me uncomfortable. "We better get you to the office as soon as possible. Do you think you can hold up for fifteen minutes?"

I nodded. Glavio stayed silent for a while before speaking again.

"I suppose you want to know who we are," Glavio assumed.

Phoenix shrugged. "Your badges make it pretty obvious."

"They do," I agreed, remembering how, earlier, when everything was blurry and confounding, I read their badges as MAD. "You're WAD: The Wizarding Agency of Defense. You help protect Arma. Were you tracking Calypso? Is that how you found out we were kidnapped?"

Glavio nodded. "Calypso is very powerful. She can control canines and use them at her will." He took a deep, bracing breath. "She has a plot to steal the Roses of Arma."

Phoenix furrowed her brow. "The Roses of Arma? Aren't those the Roses that keep wizarding magic safe? If they're destroyed—"

"Our magic dies forever." Glavio sighed, and the sagging of his eyes and struggle to stay awake surfaced clear on his face. "We thought this was her only plan, but clearly it only masks her true motives. Calypso has safehouses all across Arma. She's going to steal the Roses and destroy them so wizards will lose their magic. If this happens, then the Wizarding Agency of Defense will lack magical ability and—"

"You won't be able to protect Arma." Phoenix finished. "Not to mention, all the innocent wizards around the world would lose an important part of themselves. But why would she do that?"

"She wants to take over Arma," I whispered.

Phoenix turned her head to me with raised eyebrows. "But wouldn't getting rid of wizarding magic hurt her too? Wouldn't that affect her army if she *is* planning on taking over Arma?" she questioned.

"She said something about her army," I told Phoenix, recalling the limited conversation we exchanged, which was still more than I'd liked. "I think she was talking about her animals. I think that's what she meant by her babies."

*"Babies?"*

I shrugged, trying hard not to relive the terrifying events vividly in my mind. "Don't ask me. She said they didn't have any food at all, and were starving for something real."

Of course, I didn't mention that the 'real' thing she was talking about was Phoenix.

Phoenix frowned. "But wizards are more powerful than dogs. I mean, the entire wizarding army versus a bunch of wolves? Isn't that a bit of a long shot?"

"So you're saying she wasn't talking about her canines? But… what else could it possibly be?"

"I don't know, but it doesn't sound good."

I craned my neck to look at Glavio, who was frowning down at his hands and scrunching up his eyebrows.

"Glavio," I started slowly, "you said WAD is tracking Calypso's operation. So maybe you know why she targeted me?"

I wasn't all that surprised when Glavio responded by just shaking his head. "I'm not sure… I'm just not sure…"

He knew.

*That* much was obvious.

Phoenix and I exchanged meaningful looks but said nothing.

After uncovering this cold, harsh truth, all of us remained silent, surrounded by our own thoughts. I tried my best not to think about Calypso, for her true intentions for Phoenix made me even queasier than when I had turned around to find a man with a knife stalking me.

Calypso taking over *Arma*?

Of course, Arma had fought off many challenges in its time, but no one had ever been bold enough to go for world dominance except for once in Armanian history— Ametrine, the witch who could befriend monsters, when she started the Beast War. That had lasted for years and had had such devastating effects that no one had ever, not once, tried that again. World dominance! It sounded almost ridiculous in my mind.

I wasn't even sure whether I should believe Glavio at all.

*And* the maniacs who wanted to take over the world just kidnapped me, threatened to kill me, and nearly tortured me with a knife, which was hard enough to swallow.

"Are you okay?" A voice jutted into my thoughts. I threw my head up to see Phoenix. "You're cold and clammy."

If I was being honest, she didn't look much better either. Her face was pale, and she was squeezing her hands so hard, they were losing color.

"I'm fine," I replied quickly, concealing my feelings. I turned to Glavio. "Are we going to be getting protection from WAD? Because Calypso obviously went to great lengths to kidnap us and try to gain my support."

"It depends," Glavio admitted.

"Depends on what?" Phoenix asked. Her ears perked up as soon as I mentioned 'protection.'

"You'll see."

"Can't you just tell us?" I pressed.

"Trust me—you'll see."

The most annoying thing about Glavio was that he was hard to argue with. Once he was set on something, he moved like a rock—in other words, he didn't.

Still, questions bubbled in my head, like what was Glavio not telling us? Why did Calypso kidnap me and want me to work for her? What was Calypso's plan? And who, or what, were her babies? There were so many questions bursting in my head. For every one of them, two more popped up.

Over the last forty-eight hours, my life had turned upside down.

"Look! We're landing!" Phoenix called, pointing at the ground. Sure enough, the ground was getting closer. We were landing outside a huge building. The front entrance to it had three big letters hammered above it: WAD.

We were landing at WAD headquarters!

Even though it wasn't under the best circumstances, I couldn't stop the smallest rush of excitement.

This was *the* WAD headquarters. Practically every kid in Arma wanted to visit it. It was the most private, secure, and high-tech place that ever existed. Its location was in the middle of nowhere, and only WAD agents knew how to get to it.

"Hold on! This might be bumpy!" Glavio warned. I didn't need to be told twice. Clutching the seat, I peeked out the window to find the ground rocketing towards us at an alarming speed. I braced myself, shut my eyes in anticipation, and right when I was sure we would crash straight into the ground in a mangled heap of dead bodies, our carriage pulled up and smoothly landed outside headquarters.

"Ugh," I moaned, dizziness whooshing over me.

My slash stung, turning a nasty shade of purple.

Phoenix kicked open the door zealously, and we followed her out of the carriage. Glavio helped me down, and automatically, I leaned on a tree, taking a deep breath while attempting to steady myself.

I looked up, ready for the best.

The building was big, there was no doubt about that, and surrounding it was a sparkling purple forcefield.

Inside, there were large, tinted windows on its ends. The front entrance was large and circular. Doors lined up next to each other, each with secure, designated wand holes on them, and creatures that looked like fairies fluttered about, scanning wizards and sorceresses for suspicious items. People levitated themselves on floating hoverboards to get to doors that were fifty feet above ground. Staircases that switched where they led to zoomed across the entrance, and tubes for teleportation had lines snaking out of them. On top of that, there were guards roaming the place, all of them wearing blue robes—identical to the ones Glavio and the rest of the wizards were wearing—with wands tucked into their pockets.

It was even more magnificent than I had imagined.

"We need to get medical attention for this boy," Glavio said urgently to the wizard in the driver's seat.

The wizard hurried out of the driver's seat and looked at my injury. His expression turned anxious.

"We'll be lucky if that isn't infected. Come on, hurry up!"

"Hurry *up*?" I gasped as he trotted towards headquarters.

***

Phoenix sat to my right, and three wizards stood in front of us. My cut had healed lightning fast. The healer told me it could take a few days for the mark to go away, but

102

my leg should be fine. It was bandaged up and barely hurt at all.

"I don't believe we've been introduced," one of the wizards said. Glavio stood next to them. He studied us with an unreadable expression.

I tried to mimic him. Phoenix and I were runaways. If anyone from WAD realized that, we might be in trouble.

But then again, given everything we'd been through, would WAD realizing that necessarily be a bad thing? Would them sending us home be detrimental after what we'd gone through?

An even worse thought occurred to me: Even if I wanted to go home, would I be allowed to, considering the danger that trailed behind me?

A wizard cleared his throat apprehensively, and Phoenix elbowed me.

"My name is Seamus," I said quickly, unsure whether I wanted to add in my last name. Before I could introduce Phoenix, every eyebrow in the room went up.

I sighed. There was no avoiding it. It wasn't like I could lie to WAD.

"Seamus Brown."

"I'm Phoenix Lersaw," Phoenix said.

"Interesting," was all a sorceress said. "My name is Eliza, executive director of WAD. This is Balthazar," she motioned to the wizard on the right, "and this is Caveat. I believe you already know Glavio."

We nodded.

"I'm deeply sorry for what Calypso put you through today. Glavio explained everything Calypso told you, and we believe our suspicions were correct. For now, you must have somewhere to stay. Your pegasus, Sorin, I believe, will be there."

I stared at her. There was no—What were you doing alone in Silenia? Who are your parents? No sitting down in a room and being asked hard questions while being studied for every reaction. That was *it*?

"Glavio has volunteered to take you in until—" Eliza stopped, clearly thinking she'd said too much. "Was that all?" she asked like nothing had ever happened.

Phoenix glared at Eliza like, *Are you serious?* I was with her on that. I got that they were a very private organization and all, but obviously, Calypso kidnapped us for a reason. It was clear they knew that as well. So why try to hide it?

"Is that all you're going to tell us?" Phoenix asked very bluntly.

Eliza remained silent. Balthazar and Caveat looked highly uncomfortable.

"Of *course*," Phoenix muttered.

"What about our packs?" I asked. "And the carriage? That carriage wasn't ours, and we had all our savings in those packs!"

Caveat stepped forward. "We sent a search team to search all of Silenia, but your carriage was gone. Calypso probably took your packs when she kidnapped you."

I tried not to think about all the liens we had in our packs. "What are you going to do with us? We can't stay at a safe place forever!"

"Leave that to us," Eliza promised gently, her expression softening. "I understand you've been through a lot today, and we're going to try to piece together the parts of the mystery. But you need to relax. We're here to help." Then she gave me a warm smile.

My mistake? I believed her.

\*\*\*

Glavio's house stood on the outskirts of Leon and was three stories tall. It had six bedrooms, a living room, a library, a kitchen, eight bathrooms, a theater, a coat closet, a basement, and an attic. It was also nearly in the middle of nowhere, because wizards don't need to be near town since they can teleport to any place they'd like. A wizard who lived in Calica could go to work every day in Timnock, which is not only convenient but super useful if you have parents who live in two separate queendoms.

What surprised me the most about Glavio's house was how big it seemed, even though it was only half the size of my home. Just a few days on the run had made me realize that my previous life was a bit *too* privileged. A bit too shielded. A bit too innocent. A bit too taken for granted!

Outside Glavio's house were the stables where Sorin made himself at home straightaway. There were archery targets I could barely make out in the distance, but other than that, it was a crisp, flat field of neatly trimmed grass stretching up to the forest that Glavio's house sat next to.

I was sitting in the living room with Phoenix next to me, holding a cup of hot chocolate with marshmallows and whipped cream. Glavio was sitting on the couch across from us.

"Thanks for the hot chocolate," Phoenix said gratefully, smiling. She had a chocolate mustache with tufts of whipped cream in it. "I've never had any so good. Mom preferred cold coffee."

Phoenix froze, but Glavio didn't seem to notice anything odd. Instead, he was nodding at what Phoenix had just said.

"You can thank my sister. She left me the recipe the last time she visited, and it's been sitting in my drawer for weeks. I thought now might be a good time to put it to use." He smiled warmly.

I couldn't help but trust Glavio, despite his mysterious appearance. He was a tall and fit man who looked to be in his thirties. He had wavy black hair, basically the opposite of Scrawny. His eyes were kind but deep, and the crinkles at the edges of his eyes indicated he smiled a lot.

"Tell your sister that her hot chocolate is amazing." Phoenix sipped the chocolate again and licked her lips.

"I most definitely will." Glavio put down his steaming cup of coffee and glanced at each of us with a raised eyebrow. "In the meantime, why don't I show you to your rooms?"

"Sure," I agreed, and Phoenix nodded.

Glavio stood up, straightening his shirt and looking down at us kindly. "Follow me," he said, leading us out of the kitchen, into the entrance hall, and up marble stairs. He led us past the theater room and many more doors before stopping in front of one. He turned around and looked at Phoenix. "Phoenix, my dear, this is yours. You'll find extra clothes in the closet—hopefully, they'll fit, but if they don't, come to me and I'll fix them up nicely for you. Make yourself at home."

"Thank you," Phoenix said, nodding at him. She sent me one last, uncertain look before heading inside the room.

Glavio turned back to me. "Follow me, Seamus. Your room is down the hall."

I followed him as he led me down the hall and stopped at a second door. "This is where you'll be staying," he explained.

I stepped forward, nodded to him, and twisted the doorknob. It was a small room, but I liked it right away. There was a large, queen-sized bed in the middle. The walls were painted sky blue, except for the entire right wall, which was a wide, lengthy window, and a beautiful view of the forest peeked into the frame. Pushed against the front wall was a wooden desk, above that a white bookshelf with countless books stacked on it. On the right wall was a white door that I assumed led to my bathroom and closet. In the corner was a comfortable-looking armchair and a snuffed out fireplace next to it.

"Clothes are in the closet, so make yourself at home." Glavio said.

"Home…" I repeated, the word heaving over my heart like an anvil. I turned to Glavio. "Sir, there's something I haven't told you," I admitted, watching nervously for his reaction.

Glavio's eyes twinkled. "And what is that?"

"Phoenix and I, we… we ran away from home a few days ago, before we were kidnapped. I'm sure you were wondering why we were touring Silenia without any adults?"

"I was, in fact, not wondering," Glavio responded, looking strangely unmoved.

I waited for more, but it never came. Staring at him, I added, bewildered, "But, sir, we ran away from home. Aren't you going to return us?"

Glavio seemed to gain age in front of me. Despair filled his eyes, and I could almost see the bags form beneath his eyes. He looked like he wanted to say something, but decided against it. "Rest, Seamus. I'm sure you're tired. If you'd like to clean yourself up, the towels are in your bathroom. Once you get hungry, meet me downstairs. I have a few things to talk about with you."

Before I could push any more, what he said struck me. "Like what?"

"I think you'll have to wait until dinner to figure that out," Glavio told me. Then he made his way out of the room.

As soon as he left, I kicked the wall furiously.

Why couldn't he just give me answers *when* I asked for them?

***

It didn't take long for my annoyance at Glavio to melt away. I took a twenty-minute-long shower in hot water and now I wore new, warm clothes, sitting in a cozy kitchen with a real, hearty dinner in front of me.

It felt like forever since I had had a home.

Phoenix was stuffing herself with all the food she could eat. She had mashed potatoes on her face and had already completely destroyed her penne pasta and bread. Now she was just beginning on her soup.

I studied my food. My lima beans and mashed potatoes with gravy had disappeared, but everything else was untouched. Glavio seemed to notice because he asked, "Something wrong?"

"No," I chirped, wrestling with my instinct to scream out *YES!* "I just have so many questions."

"That's understandable." Glavio sighed and set down his fork. "There's something I haven't told you," he admitted sullenly, his eyes dropping underneath the table.

"So, you've decided to tell us?" I asked as Phoenix rolled her eyes and grumbled, *"Finally."*

The difference in our reactions almost made me laugh.

Glavio nodded. His solemnity worried me. "A few days ago, the Seer issued a prophecy. It was about you two."

The Seer was the prophecy-speaker. She lived on the Bridge, and people visited her when they wanted to find out about their future. It usually didn't help, since prophecies were so hard to understand. Most people's prophecies drove them crazy.

She rarely ever issued specific prophecies designated to one person by *herself* though. So, if she had... that was a little concerning.

I blinked, my heart pounding faster. "A prophecy? How can you be sure it's about us?"

"It mentioned water and fire in the prophecy. Your elements are water and fire, correct?" Glavio said, his sad eyes rising to meet my frantic ones.

Phoenix stared at him. "Uh… how do you know that?"

"It's how Calypso found you," Glavio explained, moving his eyes to Phoenix. "You have an aura around you that calls anyone and everyone to you. It's hard to feel unless you are taught how to."

"We have an *aura*?" I asked, puzzled.

Glavio nodded. "It's because your powers are basic elements. Anyone who has the ability to wield one of the four basic elements has an aura that can be sensed."

"How come no one ever told us?" Phoenix asked.

"No one knew," Glavio said gravely. "Like I said, it's very hard to feel if you don't learn how to sense it. Only professionals can do it."

"So, Calypso's a professional?" I asked.

"One of the best there is, and she has more professionals working for her. Listen, the prophecy mentioned a few… er, interesting things."

I resisted the urge to scream. Glavio was moving *way* too fast for my liking.

"Interesting?" Phoenix questioned. "What…"

Glavio cleared his throat.

*"When two shall split, the journey starts.*

*They must use their strength and smarts.*

*The three pillars of Arma, scattered across the land,*

*they may be sought out by making a stand.*

*Water and fire, united as one,*

*trying to see the mission done.*

*Only against the canine mother,*

*will they see how much they need each other."*

There was a moment of silence.

"What's that supposed to mean?" I finally asked, breaking the silence.

"The Roses of Arma are sometimes referred to as the Three Pillars of Arma. It is clear that you are the ones who are supposed to thwart Calypso's plans."

"But… why would you put a couple of kids in charge of something as important as this? What's the point of WAD if kids are the ones doing your missions?" I demanded, standing up.

"We are wizards," said Glavio tenderly. "In the wizarding world, when a prophecy is issued, it is only right that you step back and let fate decide your journey. It is against the wizarding code to meddle with prophecies. It's extremely important that you are the ones who go on this journey."

I sat down and put my head in my hands, unable to believe it. In three days, I had gone from being any regular kid to a runaway, and now I was expected to save the world?

Phoenix didn't say anything. She was staring at Glavio with her mouth slightly open.

Glavio must've understood how we felt, because he stood up. "I know this is a lot to take in, so I suggest both of you get a good night's sleep."

"You want us to *sleep on it*?" Phoenix asked in disbelief.

Glavio nodded. "I think that might be best for now."

I knew that wouldn't be good enough for Phoenix, and it certainly wasn't good enough for me, but Phoenix decided it wasn't worth pushing. Instead, she let out a huge yawn.

"Alright," Phoenix said. "I'm going to bed, but only because I feel like I haven't slept properly in forever. I *am* going to ask more questions," she glared at Glavio, "*many* more questions, in the morning."

When she was gone, I glanced at Glavio, wondering how this had happened to us.

Well, actually, I knew exactly how it had happened. And it all started with me.

*I* chose to run away! *I* chose to be an ungrateful loser!

All of this, this entire mess we were in, was my fault.

"How am I supposed to take this in?" I asked quietly.

Glavio shook his head. "Seamus, you don't know it yet, but you're capable of so much more than you think. You're destined to be a savior, and even if it is always a risky path in life, it's clear that's what you're meant to be."

I wasn't sure how to respond to that.

"Tomorrow, both of you will visit my armory and pick a weapon. I'll do my best to teach you how to fight."

Teach us how to *fight*? Just when you thought it couldn't get any weirder…

"Now, you better follow Phoenix's example. It's been a long day, and I'm sure you can't wait to get into bed."

He was right about that. Before I could argue, or even respond to anything he'd just said, Glavio flicked his wand and gave me a small smile and a slight wave before I hurtled like a torpedo towards my room, reaching there in under a second.

Dizziness glazed over me, but it wasn't long before my head cleared and I was staring at the door to my room.

I had to admit, that was an awesome spell.

I flung open the door and could barely stay awake long enough to change into night clothes and flop into bed. I erupted into snores not long after my head hit the pillow.

# SEVEN

**"Seamus!" Phoenix yelled,** banging on my door. "Seamus, wake up! There are gigantic blueberry muffins that you won't want to miss!"

When my eyes first fluttered open, I couldn't remember where I was. Then it all hit me. I was kidnapped and I was staying at a WAD agent's house whose name was Glavio. I was in a prophecy that said things I didn't understand. Glavio wanted Phoenix and me to train to protect ourselves because Calypso wanted me dead, or alive on her side, and basic elements have an aura.

*How am I supposed to even remember all this let alone comprehend?* I wondered to myself, still staring at the ceiling. Did I have to leave the safe, warm bed?

"Seamus!" Phoenix yelled.

"Alright, alright!" I called. "I'm coming!"

As I listened to Phoenix's footsteps fade away, I had half a mind to just stay in my bed forever without a care in the world—but gigantic blueberry muffins sounded pretty irresistible.

Besides, Glavio had promised us answers.

I threw off the blankets on my bed, slipped into my slippers, and went to the bathroom to freshen up. I gazed into the mirror, a pair of sky blue eyes staring back at me. My black hair was a mess, and drool stuck to my chin. Looking away, I turned the tap and washed my face, the soap making my skin look white and ghostly. After rinsing my face off, I grabbed the new toothbrush in the cupboard and scrubbed as hard as I could.

How would I survive with Calypso after me? How would anyone around me survive?

I gargled and spat out foamy toothpaste, splashing water on to my face. Then I left the bathroom to enter the closet and found a stack of clothes neatly folded for me. I clasped the sweatpants and shirt in my hands, changing into the soft clothes. Soon I was ready, and when I gazed at myself in the mirror, my mouth twisted into a grin. At least I looked myself again.

Almost.

But, still… it felt good.

Turning my attention away from the mirror, I hurried down the stairs and into the kitchen. Glavio was cutting vegetables on a cutting board, his knife slicing through them smoothly. Phoenix had a pile of whipped cream—no, a stack of pancakes in front of her and orange juice on her right. I rolled my eyes. Only Phoenix could eat whipped cream for breakfast.

When Glavio went to get more vegetables, he caught sight of me and smiled. "Seamus! How did you sleep?"

"Great," I answered, sliding into the seat next to him.

Phoenix grinned. "I could barely get him out of the bed," she teased, pointing a spoonful of whipped cream at me.

My face turned pink, and Glavio chortled. "That's alright. My sister isn't much of a morning person either. I set out pancakes for you, by the way. They're on the counter. And check if there's still whipped cream left in that, will you?"

"I doubt it," I muttered, but when I shook the bottle, I was stupefied to find it was full. "How is it full?"

"Magically refills," Phoenix explained.

"It seems my charm worked well," Glavio remarked, swiping all the vegetables into a large bowl.

"That explains why Phoenix is stuffing herself today." I tilted my head towards Phoenix's mountain of whipped cream as I served myself pancakes. She grinned.

"For once I can have as much whipped cream as I want, and I'm supposed to refuse that?" Phoenix shook her head as she spooned some more whipped cream. "It's so *good*."

I topped my pancakes with at least triple the amount of whipped cream I usually have. It was nowhere near as much as Phoenix had, but it was still a lot. Hey, Phoenix did have a point. In front of me was forever-lasting whipped cream, and I wasn't supposed to use it?

Glavio poured the vegetables and mixed up eggs on a sizzling pan. He turned it on medium heat, grabbed his coffee, and dropped down in an empty chair. "Today is the first day of training," he mentioned.

I nearly threw up my pancakes. "You were being serious last night?" I asked, even though I knew the answer to the question.

"I'm afraid I was being very serious, Seamus."

"I just don't get it," Phoenix said, wiping whipped cream off her face. "Why were we spoken about in the prophecy? I mean, what's so special about two regular kids from Jade?"

Glavio smiled knowingly. "What was so special about Alexander the Great before he helped Arma get rid of one of the bloodiest wars in history and defeat Ametrine, the witch who could befriend monsters? He was just a poor fellow from a struggling family. It was a surprise he went to the military at all, with his family in the state they were in. His sister sick and his father dead… Do you think he thought he'd be a hero?"

Glavio did have a point. It wasn't like Alexander knew he'd be named Founder of Arma and be the hero every kid looked up to while growing up.

"Yeah," Phoenix admitted when she finally reached the pancake part of her pancakes, and a flicker of disappointment flashed across her face, "but he wasn't rushed into it all at once. Besides, he *chose* to join the army. He wasn't mentioned in a prophecy he knew nothing about. He wasn't absolutely clueless."

"Exactly!" I agreed.

"I understand this may feel a bit *sudden* to you two," Glavio sipped his coffee and continued kindly, "but it is vitally important that both of you train as hard as you can to protect yourselves when you go on this dangerous journey. No one else can take it on but you, and if you don't, then Calypso will go through with her plan and Arma will be no more. Only you two can save Arma. The Seer has spoken."

I glanced at Phoenix, who was biting her lips. At least I wasn't the only one who thought this was way too much.

But I also knew that what Glavio said was true. No one else would be able to save Arma from collapsing if we didn't. Calypso would steal the Roses and destroy wizarding magic for good. That's when I understood the desperation and despair in Glavio's eyes. If we didn't help him, who would? That seemed like a pretty bad way to treat WAD after they'd saved our lives.

But if we failed, we would die or have to live the rest of our lives in some sort of prison of torture Calypso would force us into. And this time, based on what happened last time, Phoenix may not escape.

Not only that, but we knew nothing about fighting bad guys. We lived peaceful lives. How were we supposed to suddenly become fighters capable of taking on Calypso's vicious army?

And how much time *did* we have?

"Do you accept?" Glavio asked, sooner than I was ready to give an answer.

Did we *accept*?

No, thank you, but no. A quest that could kill both of us? Throw us down a chasm so deep it'd be days before we hit the bottom? Torture us using an evil sorcerer?

Neither of us knew *anything* about Calypso or what she could do! All I knew was that she had almost tortured me and that she wouldn't bat an eye if she had to kill me.

So why would anybody in their right mind *accept*?

I sucked in a deep breath and closed my eyes.

Despite all these thoughts cutting through my head, something inside me, a small, quiet part of me, told me to accept.

If we accepted, it reasoned, we'd be doing good in the world. We'd be helping so many people around Arma.

Not just that, but WAD protected Arma, and if WAD was gone, anything could happen.

Any number of *Calypsos* could happen.

A strong hate pounded in my heart.

I *despised* Calypso. I despised how she had decided to uproot my life. I despised how she threatened and scarred Phoenix. I despised how she relished hurting us.

But no matter how much I loathed Calypso, fear trembled inside me every time someone mentioned her. Thinking of what she could do to us, thinking of what she *almost* did to us, scared me more than anything had ever scared me before.

Some part of me wanted to kill her, but the other part wanted to curl into a ball and stay there.

But then again…

I opened my eyes.

If not us, then who?

I eyed Phoenix, my blue eyes searching her amber eyes for some sign of acceptance. She watched me intensely with so much vigor and grit, I knew what her answer was before having to ask.

I turned to Glavio, sighing, and said, "We accept."

Glavio glanced at Phoenix, who didn't argue, and then nodded, the relief that flooded across his face prominently noticeable. "Thank you, because Arma really needs your help. Since WAD already has a Rose in our possession, you will set off to find the other three of the collection when the time comes. Now hurry. The armory is inside the forest."

"Why is it there?" I asked, trying to swallow another bite.

"Some of the blades in there are so ancient and magical, people would do anything to get their hands on them."

"Great," I said, wiping the syrup of my face. "I'm thrilled."

Glavio opened the kitchen door. Phoenix, taking one last look at her pancakes, got up to follow. She gazed at me, uncertainty and fear surfacing in her eyes, but looking closer, I could see defiance and strength.

"This is a lot to take in," she admitted.

"I'm not sure if this is the right choice," I confessed, "but we have to do this, don't we?" I glanced at her for reassurance.

Phoenix nodded. "We'll figure it out."

Comforting.

She walked to the door, and I trailed behind her.

Glavio led us through the living room and out the entrance hall. He stood waiting for us by the front door. When he caught sight of us, he unlocked the front door and creaked it open.

"Come on," he said. "The trek through the forest isn't very far."

We followed him out the door and were immediately hit by a strong gust of wind. The refreshing air blew my hair to the side, as if it were trying to free itself from my head. I squinted ahead, trying to see through the sharp wind, and made out a large forest, thick with trees that towered up to what looked like fifty feet. A path wove through the brush, with occasional tree roots overriding it. It looked like it could go on forever.

"I hope he knows the way," Phoenix whispered to me, raising an eyebrow at the forest.

It was an hour's walk through the forest, and that was *with* the shortcuts. Once, a huge snake slithered by, and while Phoenix and I froze, paralyzed, Glavio stooped down, muttered something under his breath, and stroked it. The only good thing about the forest was that it was shady, so at least we'd be petrified by huge, poisonous snakes slithering by without getting a sunburn at the same time.

When we finally emerged into a clearing in the forest, I caught sight of the armory just up ahead. It was shaped like a huge greenhouse, but instead of regular, see-through glass walls to allow the sun to stream through, the armory was made of cold, dark stone. A large, wooden door with rings hanging off the doorknob was at the front.

We cut through the tall grass of the field to the armory. When we reached the door, Glavio began pulling things out of his pockets and muttering, "I know I have it here somewhere."

"You mean the key?" Phoenix asked, examining the rusted keyhole on the door.

Without looking up, Glavio nodded. Phoenix glanced at me with a raised eyebrow, and we waited for about five minutes before Glavio finally came up with a tiny, golden key that had an emerald on the end of it.

"Aha! I found it!" Glavio cried triumphantly.

"No wonder you couldn't find it," Phoenix remarked. "It's tiny."

"Yes, well, it is hard to find sometimes. The key maker who made this is an old friend of mine, and thought it'd be a funny joke. Of course, that was before he realized it was the key to the armory," Glavio explained, squinting at the keyhole. He twisted the key in, and I waited with bated breath, the anticipation building inside me, but when he pushed the door, it wouldn't budge.

Seriously?

"Does the key not fit?" Phoenix asked impatiently.

"Oh no, it fits just fine," Glavio said, frowning. "It's just, I haven't opened this door for so long. It's probably stuck. We're going to have to push it to get it unstuck."

I was outside an armory full of magical and ancient weapons, and the door was *stuck*?

Thanks for ruining the moment.

I sighed. "Alright, let's open it."

All of us leaned against the door, shifting all our weight against the rotting wood. The door screeched an inch forward, and Glavio must've felt it too, because he called out, "Come on everybody! Push harder!"

The door screeched forward another measly inch. *This is one stubborn door,* I thought as I threw myself against the door with all my might. Then the door moved a few inches, and I realized what was going to happen right before it happened.

The door flew open, sending everyone catapulting to the ground. We hit the stone floor with a loud *THUMP!* I groaned.

"Ouch," Phoenix complained, picking herself off the ground. She held out a hand to me and pulled me up onto my feet again.

"Thanks," I nodded, brushing myself off. Glavio was already off the ground, looking sheepish.

"Sorry about that," he muttered. "I'm quite disorganized for a wizard."

"That's alright," I grinned. Then I peered up, ready to be amazed, and saw the weapons.

Speechless.

This had to be the largest number of weapons I'd ever seen in the same place all at once. There was every different kind of weapon displayed around me, from daggers to swords, and spears to bows and arrows. There were polished shields and thick coats of armor.

"Wow," I whispered, awestruck. "This is just... wow."

When I glanced over at Phoenix, there was a wide grin sneaking onto her face, and her eyes were big and full of wonder.

"It's impressive," Glavio agreed. "Now choose your pick."

"How are we supposed to choose *one*?" Phoenix exclaimed. "There are *hundreds* of weapons here. I don't even know if I want a sword or bow and arrow!"

"Just look around," Glavio suggested. "I'm sure you'll find something that calls to you."

Phoenix sent him an odd look, but she turned around and wandered off. I frowned uncertainly at Glavio, who nodded encouragingly, and then I turned back to all the weapons before me. I strode through the greenhouse, examining blade after blade. When I was small, I had always dreamt of owning my very own bow and arrow, but when I held one up and stretched it as far back as I could, while aiming for the middle stone on the wall, I immediately knew it was not for me. That, and the fact that instead of hitting the middle stone that I aimed for, my arrow pierced the one six stones above it.

I quickly put it down and moved on to the next weapon. This was a five-foot-long spear with a spiky ball at the end of it. But as soon as I picked it up and attempted to swing it, I knew it was wrong. The spear felt off-balance and heavy.

I tried weapon after weapon, all turning out with the same fate – not for me. Glavio watched me from the corner, smiling. I had a feeling that this had once been him—a kid with hundreds of choices put in front of him and a person saying, "Choose."

I tried what felt like half the weapons in the greenhouse, when Phoenix came back with a small smile on her face.

"I think I've found it," she said decisively. She held a dagger with a black hilt, curved form, and a steel blade so shiny I could see my reflection in it. Phoenix looked pleased with herself.

Glavio's eyes became foggy. "A dagger? Good choice. That particular dagger is called the Dagger of Gryphon. It once belonged to royalty before it wound up in my hands."

"Oh, cool, a warrior princess," Phoenix grinned.

"It only fits the worthy," Glavio added as he watched the dagger with a keen gaze. "I have no doubt that it will work for you."

Phoenix inspected her newfound weapon. With the dagger in her hand, she looked different. There was more strength in her stance, and reading the expression on her face, it looked like she could fight the world.

Or maybe it wasn't the dagger.

Maybe it happened recently.

Phoenix turned to me before I could become fully absorbed in my thoughts. "Still looking?"

I shrugged, forcing myself not to take a step back from her glinting blade. "None of the weapons that are here fit me."

"Oh, I seriously doubt that," Glavio said casually, a twinkle in his eyes. "I have the biggest collection of weapons in the entire kingdom—Calica as well as Timnock, actually. If you can't find your weapon here, then I'm out of ideas."

I went to the back of the armory to look for more. Before I could touch a single weapon there, a shining blade caught my eye.

In the middle of a bow and a javelin was a gleaming sword. Its blade shone in the light. When I moved closer, I realized the blade looked almost golden. I breathed heavily, mystified, and reached out to hold it in my hands. To my surprise, when I held it, it wasn't as heavy as the spears I had tried—it was light and easy to carry, and not only that, but it balanced perfectly.

"Wow," I murmured, unable to pull away from its golden beauty.

"Have you found something you like yet?" Phoenix called from the other side of the armory. "If you have, let's see it."

I took the blade with me, holding it in front of me so I could admire it as it caught the light streaming through the slits high on the walls and made my way to the front of the armory, where Glavio and Phoenix stood waiting. When Phoenix saw my sword, she widened her eyes.

"Wicked," she grinned.

"Well chosen." Glavio's eyes glinted. "That's a very special blade."

I was about to say I hadn't exactly chosen it yet, but I couldn't bring myself to put it down, so I knew arguing would be pointless. Instead, I questioned, "Special?"

"That was Alexander's blade," Glavio replied pleasantly.

I nearly dropped the sword. Out of the corner of my eye, Phoenix's eyes bulged. "You're kidding." I gawked. "I'm holding something *ancient*?"

"I told you some of the weapons here are ancient and magical," Glavio responded amiably, examining the dust on a nearby javelin.

"No. Way." I held the blade in front of me with new reverence. "Does that mean it can turn into a dagger and everything?"

Glavio laughed. It was the first time I had heard him laugh, and it bounced off the walls, brightening the whole room. "Yes, it can turn into a dagger. Just think of it that way, and it'll happen."

I closed my eyes and imagined Alexander's blade shrinking into a golden dagger. When I opened my eyes, Phoenix looked awestruck, Glavio smiled like he knew everything, and instead of the sword I once carried, in my hands was a newly shrunken dagger.

"That's amazing," I croaked, marveling at the weapon in my hands. "No wonder Alexander was so great. He had *this* to fight with."

Then I closed my eyes again, and when I opened them, the dagger had grown back into the mystical sword. I shook my head, trying to believe that the sword in my hands used to be owned by my greatest hero.

"Didn't he also have a bow and arrow?" asked Phoenix abruptly.

There was a mysterious glint in Glavio's eye as he said, "I'm afraid I don't have that in my collection."

"So, are we going to learn how to use our weapons?" Phoenix said, ripping her eyes away from Alexander's sword. "Because I can't wait to try my dagger out." She swung her dagger, fighting an invisible enemy.

"There's a practice field outside my house," Glavio offered.

"That's another *hour-long* walk," Phoenix complained. "Is there any place we can go that's closer to here?"

"We *could* practice here, if you'd like," Glavio suggested, "in the large wheat field next to the armory.

I'm sure it could work since neither of you need targets for a bow and arrow."

"Sounds good," I agreed.

We left the armory, Glavio locking the door behind us. Phoenix wouldn't take her eyes off her dagger. I didn't blame her. I was inclined to do the exact same thing, but I didn't want her to admire her dagger for the rest of her life, so I nudged her and shouted, "Race you!"

Phoenix stared at me like I was crazy. "You're holding a *sword*. You'd chop my legs off, and then who would save the wizards?"

I figured she was right, so to spare her legs (and wizarding magic), I shrunk my sword into a dagger. Still amazed at what I had done, I grasped it tightly and watched Phoenix, who clutched her own dagger in her right hand.

"Three… two… one… GO!" I shouted.

We tore through the field, the long grass biting at our ankles. I've always been faster than Phoenix because my legs are longer. The wind blew my hair back as I easily outstripped Phoenix, reaching the wheat field two seconds before she did. We stopped and keeled over to catch our breath. I flashed my eyes at Phoenix with a smug grin on my face.

"I won," I reminded her.

Phoenix crossed her arms. "Gee, I didn't notice."

Glavio strode towards us. He held a silver sword that he hadn't been holding before.

"Woah, cool sword," Phoenix commented with an impressed tone.

"Nice blade," I agreed, nodding at his sword. Then I watched Glavio carefully. "Are you going to battle me with that?" I asked edgily.

A mischievous smile adorned Glavio's face. "I want to test your wit and strength. I am over your level—"

"Um, you *think*? You're *WAD*. You're gonna crush me!"

Glavio, with a small smile playing on his face, continued. "But the sword is not an easy weapon to master, especially considering your blade's history. It's not going to be easy to live up to Alexander's legend. You will have to be patient as you learn."

He knew he'd win.

*That* much was obvious.

"Thanks, I always knew you believed in me," I remarked.

"Oh, shut up," Phoenix elbowed my side.

"I'll try not to hurt you," Glavio promised, walking away from Phoenix and into the wheat field.

"Reassuring," I muttered, moving across from Glavio. He held up his sword, focus submerging his eyes, and I grew my dagger back into a sword, holding it up in front of me. "You've got to remember I've never done anything like this before," I warned, nervously eyeing his easily balanced sword.

Glavio chuckled. "I know. Are you ready?"

I sighed. It was going to be embarrassing being pulverized by Glavio, but I didn't have much of a choice.

"Ready."

He lunged at me, sword out. Instinctively, I rolled to the side and kicked him. Then I realized that probably wasn't allowed, but before I could shout out an apology, he whirled around. Caught by surprise, I barely managed to duck before his sword took my head off. I swiped at him, but he deflected it easily and took a spin at me. I swung my sword at his spin, but Glavio dodged with a quick duck, sprang up, and brought his sword down on mine, catapulting it across the field.

"Hopping kangaroos, you're good!"

I was shoved to the ground, sweat pouring off of me. I wasn't thinking about the fact that Glavio had just complimented me, or the fact that he had just said 'hopping kangaroos.' I was thinking about how he had almost killed me.

I glared at Glavio angrily. "Are you *crazy*? You could've killed me!"

Glavio's smile disappeared. "I'm sorry, Seamus, but I had to make sure you believed death was close. Though, under the pressure, you did well. You've never fought with a sword before?"

"I wouldn't have agreed to this if I'd known that my life was on the line in one measly practice sword fight."

"My sword can't do any real damage... it's just for training," Glavio said quietly.

Ice spread from my spot. My cheeks flushed bright red, and I closed my eyes, forcing the ice to melt.

Ugh.

Losing control over your powers was *so* for novices.

"Sorry," I muttered, looking down.

"Don't be." Glavio shook his head, a fascinated expression dawning on his face. "How long have you known about your powers, Seamus? Icing is advanced for someone with water powers."

"Phoenix and I have both known about it since we were five," I explained, turning to Phoenix who was approaching us, nodding. "We've been training together forever."

"Five? That's an early age."

"We discovered our powers accidentally. There was a fire in a restaurant we were eating at. I tripped and fell in, but the fire didn't hurt me. And then, a few months later, Seamus was swimming in a pool, but when he went under, he realized he could breathe normally. He was only able to do it for the first time then," she added.

"Makes sense," Glavio agreed. "There's always the breaking age where your power decides to show itself. It's different for everyone."

I nodded. "So, we've been training ever since then. I learned how to ice a year ago."

"Then both of you must be decent with your powers," Glavio guessed, holding out a hand to me and helping me up.

Phoenix shrugged. "We know how to use them to our advantage, I guess."

"Maybe, in the evening before dinner, you could show me what you can do?"

I shrugged, a bit taken aback. "Sure."

"Fantastic," Glavio smiled. "Now, back to training. Phoenix, I believe I have some dummies inside the armory. Take those out, and you can practice on them. I'm going to continue working with Seamus over here, if that's alright." He tossed her the key.

"Alright," Phoenix replied, catching the tiny, golden key. She took off towards the armory, tearing through the snapping wheat with her dagger in hand.

I regarded Glavio, wondering what was in store for me next. But Glavio just smiled at me pleasantly. It was impossible to stay mad at him for long.

"Seamus, you have much potential in becoming a talented sword fighter. I have a feeling that you'll become a great warrior one day, but there are some things you need to work on to get started. First of all, never loosen your grip in the middle of a sword fight. That can be costly, as you saw before."

I nodded.

"You always want a Seminar grip. It gives you the best control and hold. Of course, this is the most basic grip, and I'm sure you're going to be learning better, more advanced grips soon."

"But I only just started," I protested.

"Ah, you're a natural." Glavio waved his hand. "I have my full confidence in you. But never drop your guard. Sword fighting isn't for the lazy. It's for the precise, the vigilant. You always have to be up for it. Never drop your guard, because this can result in your own bloody death."

"I'm liking this more and more."

Glavio smiled. "Don't worry. For now, here's the last thing: Never get desperate. Getting desperate in a sword fight can also result in your own bloody death. If you can't find openings to attack, keep up with your defense and tire your opponent out, but stay watchful. You need tense reflexes to be good at this."

"So never loosen your grip, always keep up your guard, and never get desperate," I repeated, counting each one off on my fingers. "Aren't those all basically the same thing?"

"To the untrained eye, perhaps," Glavio admitted, "but as you carry on, you will realize the significance and individuality of each of these rules. It's crucial you learn the basics before fighting."

Phoenix banged open the door of the armory dragging two dummies behind her. She waved at us. Glavio smiled. "Found them, did you?"

She nodded. We watched her set them up for a minute and bring out her dagger. She glared at the dummies reproachfully before stabbing one and slicing the other's arm off. I gaped at her. Phoenix had a *dark* side?

Glavio turned back to me. "Oh, and one more thing."

I frowned, blinking at him. "What?"

"Never attack someone from behind unless that person is a real toad, got it? Be a person of honor, even in a fight to death."

"So, I can't stab Calypso from behind?"

Glavio smiled.

I grinned. "I'll do my best," I promised. *I'd anyways like to look in her evil eyes when I defeat her,* I thought.

"Alright." Glavio raised his sword once again. "I want you to try defense. When I swipe my sword at you, raise your sword like this," he demonstrated, "and use all your strength to push me back. This is one of the most simple techniques, but it is also one of the most effective."

"Hyah!" Phoenix shouted from the corner, beheading a dummy.

I glanced at the sword in my hand. I was about to learn how to use it. I was about to learn how to really fight.

And somehow, I knew I was ready.

# EIGHT

**Well, I was anything _but_ ready.**

Weeks passed, and I can't say life was easy. Every night for the next several weeks, I crept into my bed bruised, exhausted, and dispirited. Usually, we started each day early in the morning, eating the omelets Glavio cooked. Gone was the inexhaustible can of whipped cream because, according to Glavio, "Fighters need healthy, wholesome food, not fluff in their body."

Then we would run through the forest to the training grounds near the armory. Our warm-up left us breathless from the very start. After reaching the field, Glavio took us through an exercise program to strengthen our muscles. We'd take a short break, where Glavio tried to get us into the 'wonders of meditation' to build up focus.

After that, Glavio spent hours on end practicing sword fighting with me. He yelled out criticism and encouragement as our blades clinked against each other. He taught me balance and posture. Footwork and economy of hand movements. He taught me how to use my eyes, how to position my head, and how to avoid false moves. He was ridiculously good and beat me like a ragdoll nearly every day, so I woefully prepared myself for humiliation at the beginning of each practice. Then he left me training advice to practice while he trained with Phoenix. We'd take a bit to rest for lunch, sometimes watching each other's training. We would end the day sprinting through the forest again. We would reach Glavio's house dirty, exhausted, and bruised all over. Some days, Glavio squeezed in time to practice our powers. Turns out, neither of us were *anywhere* near as good as we thought. As the weeks passed, I could feel our improvement. In the beginning, what took us forty minutes to run through now took us twenty. I was holding up against Glavio way better. My humiliation at least turned into a fight, even though I lost more often than not. Phoenix now moved like an agile cat, spinning an invisible web around her opponent.

One morning, after my sword practice was over, Glavio called Phoenix over to join us. I flopped on the grass, pouring water over my hair and face, and breathing like a dog that had just run ten miles. Phoenix dropped down next to me and rolled her eyes.

"Seriously? You have *no* stamina."

I propped myself up with my elbows and raised an eyebrow at her. "Says the girl who ran screaming from a *skunk*."

"It looked like a bear from far away!" protested Phoenix defensively.

"Kids." Glavio clapped his hands to get our attention. The gesture instantly reminded me of a kindergarten class, which is not a great feeling after sword fighting for four hours.

"Yeah?" Phoenix and I asked simultaneously.

"We have a week left of training." My nerves started swimming at the thought of facing Calypso in seven days. "The two of you have made tremendous progress since you first arrived, but there is still some work to be done. We need to discuss your battle strategies."

"Battle strategies?" I echoed. "But isn't that what we've been doing? For hours, every day? Every single day? With hardly a fifteen-minute break?"

Amusement danced in Glavio's eyes. "We've been making sure you're ready to fight *physically*. But your opponents are all going to be much bigger and stronger than you. You'll have no chance of winning—"

"Pep talk of the year," I muttered under my breath as Phoenix told me to shut up.

"—without battle strategies," Glavio finished, raising an eyebrow at me. "The best warriors learn to turn their weaknesses into their strengths. You two have had a disadvantage from the very start. Two twelve-year-olds against fighters who have been training their entire life."

"So what do we do?" Phoenix asked.

"Your opponents will see this disadvantage from the very start as well," Glavio said. "There's a good chance that they will underestimate you. And that will be your advantage."

His plan pieced together in my mind.

"Especially you, Phoenix." Glavio looked directly at Phoenix. I didn't completely understand, but Phoenix must've because she wore a sour expression.

"Because I'm a girl," Phoenix assumed bitterly.

"Huh?" I blurted.

"But they'll be making a mistake, won't they?" said Glavio gently.

Phoenix nodded resolutely. "A big one."

"You are a fast and cunning fighter, Phoenix. You know exactly where to hit them to make them crumble." Glavio continued firmly, "You will be able to quickly assess their strengths and weaknesses, while they will only see a twelve-year-old girl. If you use this to your advantage, along with your wit and agility, I'd say Calypso's minions are not going to stand a chance." Glavio paused to let that sink in. "However, the two of you must work as a team. Two are more powerful than one. You have a solid chance together. But if you must split up—" Abruptly, Glavio stopped. His eyes moved to me, sitting on the grass. "Seamus," he said quietly, "follow my plan for a moment, will you?"

Disconcerted, I glanced at Phoenix, who shrugged.

"Seamus." Glavio looked at me with solemn blue eyes that told me more than words ever could.

"There might be a time when you and Phoenix may have to split up and one has to take on a task with greater danger, a stronger opponent."

"You want Phoenix to fight the big guys," I muttered reproachfully.

With a note of surprise in his tone, Glavio said, "I want you to be the one who decides which one each of you fights. In a situation where you have to choose, I trust you to be levelheaded and have no bravado."

"More than Phoenix?"

"In this situation… yes."

The thought knocked the air out of me.

How could I do that? Put my best friend at a greater risk by *choice*?

"You need to do this," Glavio said. "You will need to in order to win. I need to be able to trust you."

*No,* everything inside me said. *No.*

But the words that left my lips were, "You can depend on me, Glavio."

***

When I opened the door to my room two days before we left for our quest, I found Phoenix sitting on the bed nonchalantly. I almost screamed. *"What the heck?"* I glowered at her.

She frowned, gandering up. "What?"

"Don't you know how to knock?"

"You weren't in here, genius." She polished her dagger and examined her reflection in it.

"If I'm not in here, maybe don't come in at *all*, genius," I told her, annoyed.

Phoenix looked away from her dagger. Her eyes were intense. Ignoring my irritation, she said, "We're stopping Calypso, aren't we?"

"That's what we've been hard-core training for, right? The prophecy said that we're the ones who have to do it… and I don't like Calypso's plans. Weakening Arma sounds…" I sighed, "really scary."

Phoenix nodded, gazing at the bedcovers. "I just… I can't believe we're doing this—for real."

"I know what you mean," I admitted, sitting down next to her. "But even if we die—which we won't," I added quickly. Phoenix smirked. "I mean, even if we do die, isn't dying trying to save Arma—dying fighting—better than

144

sitting back and doing nothing, knowing we're the ones who are supposed to do it? Knowing that we're the only ones who could've made a difference, change the world for the better, but we gave up without even trying?"

Phoenix pondered it for a minute.

"You're right," were the words that finally came out of her mouth. Her voice shaky, but her eyes looked determined.

I grinned.

"Well, anyway," Phoenix stood up from the bed. "See you in the morning."

"Goodnight," I called as she left the room.

When I heard the door click close, I ambled to the window, resting my head in my palms as I studied the night. Stars blinked down at me as if they were dancing, and the moon hung above, shining down on Glavio's home. I'd never seen so many stars out before, each one glistening brilliantly.

The thing that surprised me most, though, was that my selfish, bratty self believed in himself.

# NINE

**Our last day at Glavio's** was nothing like our first. No one talked much. Everyone was keenly aware of the dangers ahead. Even Glavio's famous whipped cream pancakes, which we were eating for the first time in a month, couldn't cheer anyone up—not even Phoenix.

We took it easy that day, but that doesn't mean we stopped training. By now, I was beating Glavio, a trained WAD agent, about as often as not. I gotta admit, I felt proud.

After my sword practice, I watched Phoenix beat up a dummy with her dagger, and Glavio shouted out criticism and encouragement while she swiped its arms off. I'm never going to tell Phoenix this, but she was seriously impressive.

Maybe there was a chance we were ready.

Lunch was potato soup, salad, stew—a feast. It was nice to have a good meal the day before being sent off to doom.

The weird thing was, Glavio still seemed hesitant and unsure, like he *still* wasn't telling us something. But, for some reason, I never asked. Maybe I was afraid that whatever he wasn't saying would be too much for me. Maybe I was afraid of the truth.

After lunch, Glavio pulled me aside, his eyes full of concern. "I just want you to remember, Seamus, this may be the start of your journey, but that doesn't mean that, if you make it to the end of this quest, it's the *end* of your journey."

"What are you talking about?" I asked, feeling sick at the thought of his use of the phrase 'if you make it to the end.'

"The truth isn't going to be easy, and it will come to you in pieces. You will have to stay patient and strong," Glavio warned me.

"Okay," I muttered apprehensively.

Glavio didn't look completely satisfied, but he decided not to push it anymore, which I was grateful for. "Don't forget your end goal, alright? No matter how tempting it may be, no matter who is put on the end of a sword, you *cannot* forget your end goal."

Glavio's penetrating glare was so deep, it took all my willpower not to look down. "Do you understand, Seamus?"

I nodded.

Glavio relaxed. "Alright. Now back to training. I'm going to be helping Phoenix with her technique, but you can still work on a few of my dummies."

Just like that, he was back to being the same old Glavio.

At the end of the day, Glavio said he had official WAD work to do, so dinner would be later than usual. As soon as he left, I seized Alexander's sword in dagger form and trudged outside. I could hear Phoenix practicing on the field. I pictured her slicing a dummy's head off, and the thought brought a smile to my face.

I kept on moving forward, into the overgrown forest. Glavio had warned us not to go into the forest alone, but I was confident I knew the way. Besides, I needed some time alone to clear my head.

The forest's trees cast long shadows that stretched farther than I could see. I watched squirrels hop from stump to stump and bobcats chase after rabbits. The bobcat fixed its eyes on me, its eyes piercing through me. A few weeks ago, I probably would've cowered, but Alexander's dagger reassured me. I calmly kept my hand on its hilt, watching the bobcat with a raised eyebrow. Finally, it turned away and pounced after the rabbits.

It was an hour before I emerged on the other side of the forest. I squinted to my right and noticed the sea cliff I had come for. The sea was calm and soothing today, nipping at the shore quietly. The tranquil waves were peaceful and relaxing.

I jogged to the cliff. The sun dipped slowly below the horizon. A pod of dolphins swam, visible in the distance, right below the bright, orange sun. I grinned.

A voice made me jump. "Is the view good over there?"

Without turning around, I exclaimed, *"Phoenix!* Don't sneak up on me like that!"

Phoenix rolled her eyes as she plopped down next to me.

We both sat there, watching the sun sink slowly beneath the ocean. This was how it all started—at a sea cliff, watching a sunset—before we decided to run away. Another start to another adventure.

*One's enough for me,* something rumbled in my head.

Phoenix drew a smiley face in the dirt with her dagger. Grinning, she turned to me. "So… wanna jump in?"

*"What?"*

"Come on. You drove the carriage to Silenia, remember? That was super high up. So high up you could barely see the ground."

"Of course, I could see the ground. It was the only thing I looked at half the time."

"Still. How is that any different from a sea cliff only a few feet off the sea? You've got to love the sea."

"I *do* love the sea. I *don't* love heights."

"Don't be stupid. It'll be fun."

"No."

"Want me to push you in?"

"*Phoenix,*" I scowled, "I came here for some peace and quiet before the quest. I came here to listen to the waves and calm down. So, I would greatly appreciate it if you *shut up.*"

Phoenix groaned, but she didn't say anything. I let out a little sigh as I watched the sun sink lower and lower.

The dolphins disappeared beneath the surface as the sun finally dispersed under the ocean. Stars twinkled in the night sky, and a crescent moon shone brightly above us. For once, Phoenix didn't say anything. She just sat there, gazing up at the stars.

Of course, it was too good to last. "Now can I talk?"

Even surprising myself, I laughed. "It doesn't matter anymore. We better get going. Glavio's going to be done with his work, and when he finds out we went into the forest without him, he'll go ballistic." The worst thing that could happen would be Glavio getting mad at us the night before the quest.

"I don't think Glavio's the type to go ballistic," Phoenix remarked, throwing a stone into the ocean.

I rolled my eyes. "You know what I mean."

Phoenix stood up, grinning. "Race you."

I almost laughed out loud. "After I beat you by a mile last time? I would've thought you didn't have the guts."

Phoenix's eyes glinted dangerously. "How about…" She grasped her dagger. I was almost afraid she was going to gut me with it, but she turned her attention towards the ocean. An all too evil smile appeared on her face. "If I win this race, you have to jump off a sea cliff somewhere."

"Somewhere?"

Phoenix shrugged. "Maybe we'll find time during our quest."

"Probably not," I muttered under my breath. Luckily, Phoenix didn't hear. She had already turned around, ready to bolt.

"What happens if I win?"

"Then you have a dare," she responded, focusing her eyes on the forest.

Since when was Phoenix so confident that she could beat me? I *always* beat her in races. It was one of the things that I mentioned every day just to annoy her.

I stretched into my running position, my eyes stuck on the path straight ahead. My nerves tingled as Phoenix's newfound confidence made me ponder whether Glavio had given her an acceleration potion.

"Three… two… one… *GO!*"

We both took off, sprinting through the trees of the forest. Now I understood why Phoenix was so confident. The path was narrow, and hard for both of us to get through. There were roots on the ground ready to trip you once you came close, and branches hung low, meaning we had to duck to get through. The truth was, Phoenix wasn't faster than me in a straight race on flat, easy ground, but she was more agile when we had to jump, dodge, and duck while making ground.

It was also a big forest. About twenty-five minutes run to the armory and another fifteen to the house. A month of training had left me sure-footed. I could run at a good pace with great stamina. I kept my eyes on the path, dodging tree trunks and jumping over roots. Unfortunately, the branches that hung low were a real problem. Ducking them took a great amount of my energy.

My chances of winning just shrunk by a lot.

An idea popped into my head. Hoping it would work for my own sake, I grasped Alexander's sword, which was shrunken into a dagger at the moment, and imagined it growing. The dagger grew into a gleaming sword. I grinned and held it above my head, letting its flat side launch the branches out of my way. It still took energy, but not nearly as much as ducking had before.

But of course, Phoenix realized how helpful that would be and clasped her own dagger. It didn't work as well as a sword, but unfortunately for me, it still worked.

I was confident enough that neither of our arms would get tired, what with the amount of pushups we did a day, but I was still relieved when the trees changed and grew tall enough for none of the branches to be low enough to affect us.

We'd been racing for what felt like forever, me a bit ahead of Phoenix. The forest grew dark. *Glavio will be home soon,* I realized, and I instantly felt guilty. He'd be worried out of his mind if he found his home empty. The thought pushed me to run even faster.

Soon enough, I could make out the open field next to Glavio's house near the end of the forest. Except…

Like magic, Phoenix streaked past me. I bolted after her desperately, cutting through the greenery and brush as fast as I could, but it was too late. Phoenix tumbled out of the forest. When she stood up, she grinned, and I groaned, stopping right next to her.

"That was *so* unfair," I stormed.

The victorious smile on Phoenix's face didn't disappear. "Such a sore loser," she said in a pitying way and sent me a mocking smile. I wanted to kill her. "Know what this means? A cliff somewhere is waiting for you."

Before I could come up with a response, Glavio's familiar voice shouted, "Kids! What are you doing out there?"

Phoenix and I exchanged looks before darting to where Glavio stood. I couldn't read his face, but there were bags under his eyes, and he drooped, his shoulders slouching. He looked like he could pass out on the spot.

"What happened at work, Glavio?" I frowned.

"Yeah, you look like you just climbed Mount Everest," Phoenix commented as she surveyed Glavio with her eyebrows creased. "No offense," she added quickly as her cheeks tinged.

"Nothing happened... Nothing at all..."

Phoenix raised her eyebrows at me and gestured towards Glavio. I knew exactly what she was thinking.

Glavio was *still* hiding things from us, even things that were increasingly obvious by the second.

"Can you just tell us already?" I asked him, a little more harshly than intended. "Something's definitely up. Spill."

Glavio sighed. "Inside, both of you."

Before either of us could respond, Glavio turned his back on us and rushed inside. Having no choice but to follow him, we trailed behind him as he led us into the living room and gestured towards the seats. Reluctantly, we both sat.

"Hot chocolate?" Glavio asked weakly.

"Later," I stated, crossing my arms. "Glavio, what's going on at work? Is it about Calypso and the Roses?"

Glavio looked down. "I hate to tell both of you this, but… I've been suspended from the Wizarding Agency of Defense."

*"What?"* we both exclaimed, completely bewildered.

"Why would they do that?" Phoenix clamored.

"That's private Wizarding Agency of Defense matters," Glavio responded sharply. Phoenix stepped back. I couldn't blame her. Glavio hardly ever raised his voice, even at the rabbits who constantly ate out of his garden.

"Okay," Phoenix mumbled.

Glavio gave his head a shake. "I'm sorry, Phoenix. Today has been stressful, but your quest is tomorrow. I suggest you eat a hearty dinner and get a good night's sleep. In the morning, I'll fill you in on everything you need to know for the quest."

I frowned. "But… what do we need to know?"

Glavio smiled, and the familiar old dimples returned. "Didn't I just say I'd fill you in on everything in the morning? Now come on, it's time you got some rest."

***

When I woke up the next morning, rays of sun shone through the window. I glanced at the clock on my bedside table. It was seven, but my head was still woozy and my shoulders still drooping. Still, I looked forward to another day of sword practice and learning how to use my skills.

That's when I remembered.

I groaned, throwing the covers off me. As soon as I managed to get myself out of bed, there was a knock on my door.

"Seamus! We're waiting for you downstairs. We have to leave soon if we want to stop—" Phoenix stopped suddenly. Quieter, she continued, "If we want to save wizarding magic."

My eyes still half closed, I pulled myself up. Then I called out, "I'm coming down! Just give me a few minutes."

It was easy to picture Phoenix rolling her eyes as she left my room. I slouched into the shower and washed myself in record time. Then I grabbed my toothbrush, zoomed it around my mouth for two minutes, and headed out of the room.

Downstairs, instead of everyone being relaxed in the kitchen like usual, Phoenix and Glavio were standing up, pacing, each holding similar bags. When Phoenix caught sight of me, she handed me a croissant.

"Hurry up, slowpoke. We have to get going soon," she warned.

"Good morning to you, too," I retorted, taking a huge bite out of my croissant. My stomach rumbled for more. Phoenix gave me a look that said, without question, *Boys*.

"Here's your pack, Seamus," Glavio told me, handing me a blue backpack. "Inside of it is a fresh pair of clothes, a map of Arma, toiletries, ten liens, and a bit of arius."

"Arius?" I asked quizzically.

"Eating it gives you strength during a battle," Phoenix explained quickly. "Too much of it will weaken you, and in the end, explode you to pieces."

Awesome.

"If you ever get in trouble out there, shout *Alenia*," Glavio instructed severely. Too often, I found him solemn as a priest, and at other times, his same, old, enjoyable self, like he had split personalities. "It will transport you to somewhere safe. But be warned, she only offers her services once."

"She?"

Glavio waved his hand impatiently. "The healer."

I swallowed, trying to soak it all up.

"Sorin is in the stables," Glavio continued. "You can use my carriage to travel on your quest."

"But… where are we even going to go?" Phoenix queried. "We don't know where the Roses are!"

"I'd say, look in a book," Glavio suggested. "My library has long since had nothing on the subject, but there is a book that knows where the Roses are. It's not going to be easy to find, however."

"Do you know which city it's in?" I asked.

"It's in the biggest library in Trenton," he said. "The book is called *Powerful Artifacts of Arma*. Trust me, it's not going to be in plain sight."

Phoenix nodded. "So, our first stop should be Trenton," she concluded.

Glavio nodded. "If you manage to retrieve all the Roses—"

I coughed loudly.

"*When* you manage to retrieve all the Roses," Glavio corrected, "bring them back here, and I'll return them to the Wizarding Agency of Defense headquarters."

"Okay," Phoenix agreed.

"Come," Glavio offered, walking towards the exit of the living room. "I'll help you get Sorin secured in the carriage."

We followed him out, our nerves squirming and threatening to escape, across the practice field and to the back of the house. Once we emerged outside, Phoenix's mouth split into a wide grin, and she rushed to a small, brown horse who munched lazily on hay inside his stable.

"Sorin!" Phoenix exclaimed. Sorin neighed with delight, glad to see his old friends again. Phoenix stroked Sorin fondly.

"Lead him outside, Phoenix, will you? The carriage is around back."

Phoenix opened the stable door and led Sorin out of the stables. As soon as he got out, he flapped his wings dramatically. This time, however, Phoenix dodged his wings by ducking and laughing as she stood up, leading Sorin towards the back of the stables.

The carriage waited patiently for us behind the stables. It wasn't fancy, like the ones Mr. Koren had. It was just plain brown, with sturdy structures and cushions for the seat. In some places, the wood had chipped, and the bland decor drooped. It didn't exactly look cozy, but it was our ride to Trenton and to all the other Roses.

"You better secure Sorin, now. And have a safe trip, understand? I don't want any of you coming back without arms or legs—"

"Great," I grumbled, beginning to feel sick, "you're making us feel a lot better now. Thanks for that."

Glavio cracked a smile.

"Sorin's secured," Phoenix called out. I jogged to where she was, and when I reached, I immediately clambered in. Phoenix blinked. "I guess I'll drive first, then."

"Oh, sorry," I apologized sheepishly. "If you want I could—"

"No, it's fine," Phoenix interrupted, taking Sorin's reins. "It's my turn, anyway."

I shrugged.

"Close the door, or else it'll go flying during take-off," Phoenix warned.

"Thanks for the warning, because I definitely was going to leave it open while we were hundreds of feet up in the sky."

"Just saying. You aren't exactly known for being *responsible.*"

"Since *when?*"

Glavio strode to the carriage. He smiled a bit sadly, causing my heart to sink, and making me wonder if he thought these would be the last moments he ever shared with us. I shivered slightly.

*Positive thoughts,* I reminded myself.

*Okay, here's one: We're being sent off on a potentially fatal journey against a super powerful villain who wants us dead. We don't know where the Roses are—the one thing that might save the world. The entire fate of Arma is in our hands, so if we fail, basically, everyone dies. Oh, whoops, those aren't positive thoughts. That's the reality!*

"Hold on," Phoenix shouted. Then she pivoted around and called, "Bye, Glavio! Thanks for everything!"

"Yeah, thanks!" I shouted. Then I remembered Glavio's warning. *No matter how tempting it may be, no matter who is put on the end of a sword, you cannot forget your end goal.* My heart weighed slightly as the grievous moment replayed in my head, but I yelled, "And I won't forget!"

I wasn't sure if Glavio would understand what I was talking about, but clearly, he did, because he nodded and smiled. "Good luck on your journey!"

Then I took one last look at Glavio's kind smile and sorrowful eyes before we were off, away from Glavio's comforting, safe home and into a large world full of the unknown.

\*\*\*

We made one stop at Evergreen. By that time, it was getting dark again. I tossed an apple (out of the bushel of apples in the back, since Glavio thought of everything) to Phoenix, who fed it to Sorin. Then she spread a blanket over Sorin, who was ready to rest for the night.

She joined me in the back. "So… got any spare cushions?"

I peeked under the cover. Sure enough, there were two sets of cushions. "Over here," I called, throwing her two cushions.

She set them up on the seat, and then lay down. I lay down on the floor again. "Goodnight," I mumbled, before falling asleep.

\*\*\*

It was only a few hours after I sunk into a dreamless sleep when trouble came. *BANG!* I sat straight up in my makeshift bed and clasped Phoenix's hand, which hung over the side of the seat.

She jolted awake and scowled down at me. "*What*, Seamus?"

I looked at her with wide eyes. She opened her mouth to say something that probably wasn't very nice when the noise came again: *BANG! BANG!*

Phoenix's mouth abruptly stopped midway. Her eyes widened, and she whispered so quietly I could barely hear, "Seamus… Seamus, what… what is that?"

I shook my head, my face pale. "I… I don't—"

Phoenix hissed, "Do you reckon it's… is it Calypso?"

I barely nodded. "We need to wake up Sorin and get out of here."

Phoenix unsheathed her dagger. *BANG! BANG!* The determined look on her face faltered. I seized Alexander's sword and grew it back into the golden-lit sword that was hopefully going to get us out of this situation.

"On three," I declared, holding up my fingers. "One… two… *now!*"

Phoenix kicked the door open and jumped out, me leaping out behind her. I held my sword up defiantly, ready to fight anything and everything that got in our way, but as soon as we got out, I nearly dropped it.

It was dark outside, so I could barely make out the figures advancing on us, but they were there. We were surrounded by what looked like wisping shadow monsters, with claws as sharp as Phoenix's glinting dagger.

"What the—" Phoenix started.

A shadow lunged at her, nearly stopping my heart then and there, but luckily, she swiped at it with her dagger. It disintegrated into a wisp of shadow. Phoenix turned to me, her expression unreadable.

"I just did that," she whispered, her face pale.

"How are we supposed to fight *shadows?*" I breathed.

But before Phoenix could spare another moment, a shadow monster appeared again, and two other shadows lunged at her, clearly not happy that she had just pulverized one of their friends. I raced to help her, slicing one in half, disintegrating it. Phoenix stabbed the other in the gut, but when she did, part of the shadow touched her hand.

Her hand grew so cold I could practically feel it from where I was standing. Before my eyes, it slowly began turning into a black shadow. I gasped, horrified, but luckily, when Phoenix flexed her fingers, it returned to normal.

*Breathe, breathe, breathe... She's okay, Seamus... breathe!*

"My *hand...*" Phoenix whispered as I swiped at an approaching shadow.

"Don't touch any of them," I warned, slicing another one. "Touching a shadow monster can be fatal!"

Phoenix nodded, still staring at her hand with trepidation. Finally, she jerked away and joined the fight, both of us swiping and ducking, trying our best to stay alive.

But there were just too many of them. For every one I killed, two more seemed to pop up. Phoenix wasn't having much luck either. No matter how many we killed, more shadows kept coming.

I ducked, tumbling out of the way as two shadows grabbed at me, and slicing my sword through them while narrowly dodging another attack from a different shadow.

"We can't keep it up for much longer!" Phoenix shouted. She was at the front of the carriage, battling three at once. Sorin was somehow still asleep, snoring softly in a horse dream. "There's got to be another way to escape!"

"Do you think we could just fly away?" I shouted, but just as I said it, a shadow catapulted over my head and landed onto the carriage. Almost immediately, shadows spread over the chipped wood.

"No!" Phoenix screamed. "Seamus, cover me! I need to get Sorin away from the carriage!"

I raced over there, sliding down next to her. "Go!" I shouted, slicing as fast as I could. Sweat poured off me. There was no way I was going to last another thirty seconds.

"Come on, come on," Phoenix muttered, fumbling with the hook. By now, Sorin had woken up, and he was bucking nervously, trying to get up. "No, Sorin, you have to stay still for me to help you!"

"Almost done?" I pleaded as a shadow barely missed my arm.

"And… there!" Phoenix threw the attacher off of Sorin just as shadows overtook it.

"Grab your knife!" I ordered. "We're going to fly away on—"

"*Seamus!*" Phoenix's voice shouted shrilly. I whirled around to find Phoenix on the ground, shadows spreading from her stomach. Above her was a shadow monster, claws out.

"*Phoenix!*"

Rage swept through me. I lunged at the monster, slashing Alexander's sword through him. He dissipated with a hiss, and I crouched down next to Phoenix, shadows approaching from all ends. Fear and guilt made my vision blurry and caused my hands to shake as I held her. Her amber eyes disappeared, and only the whites of her eyes were visible. She was barely breathing.

I remembered what Glavio said: *If you ever get in trouble out there, shout Alenia. It will transport you to somewhere safe. But be warned, she only offers her services once.*

I clutched Sorin's mane and held on tightly to Phoenix, swallowing the fear in my throat.

"*Alenia!*" I screamed.

Then everything went black.

# TEN

**The first thing I noticed** when I woke up was the delicious aroma of a well-cooked meal. My eyes fluttered open, and in front of me I found a tray piled with scrumptious food. Mashed potatoes with gravy, thick stew that made my mouth water, and cheesy lasagna.

Then I remembered what happened.

Slowly, I placed the tray down next to the couch I slept on. It looked like I was in the living room of a cozy home. A lit fire radiated heat in front of me; there was a small table with a vase of roses flourishing and a portrait of the royal castle in Gryphon hanging about the fireplace. I rose, treaded to the doorway, and peered around the corner of the hall to find Phoenix enjoying an identical meal to the one on my tray. I let out a huge breath when I saw her.

"*Phoenix!* You're alright." I whispered, completely devitalized.

Phoenix caught sight of me and smiled weakly. "How'd you sleep?"

I grimaced. "Like I ran a hundred miles."

"Yeah, I know," Phoenix sighed, setting her fork down in despondency. "Hestia says you got it worse because first time transportation is enervating, and you transported both me and Sorin.. She also said that I should be good as new by evening."

"Hestia?"

"The healer."

As if on cue, a woman appeared at the doorway. My mouth fell open. The woman was *strikingly* beautiful. It was impossible to take my eyes off her. She wore a plain, white apron and a blue dress, with her features standing out boldly in the light. Flowing brown hair reached her waist. Her beguiling brown eyes caught sight of me, and she gave me a warm smile.

"Hello, Seamus. You're up."

"Are you Hestia?"

In my defense, my mind was still foggy from hours of debilitating sleep.

"Always asking the obvious." Phoenix grinned, but when her eyes turned to Hestia, a look of envy flickered across her face, evaporating as fast as it came.

Hestia nodded, coming closer to us. Then, she turned back to Phoenix with a grave expression on her face. "Phoenix, my dear, I despise being the one who tells you this, but take this as only a warning."

"A... warning? What do you...?"

"There's worse things coming your way than shadow wounds. I think... they targeted you on purpose."

Phoenix exhaled sharply. "But... why would they do that?"

"You have so much warmth inside you—they knew you'd survive. I suspect that your power is fire?"

Phoenix nodded.

"Calypso wanted you to know the dangers of the quest you're going on. Glavio told me," Hestia explained to our mystified faces. "She wants to scare you off while you've barely started."

Phoenix furrowed her eyebrows. "But where would Calypso even get shadow monsters?"

"We'll have to figure it out after we save the Roses," I intervened. "We don't have enough time to keep stopping. Calypso's been after the Roses for a while now. We're lucky she's been focused on stopping us, but she definitely knows we escaped. Now she's probably going full on for the Roses."

Phoenix nodded, then turned to Hestia. "When's the soonest I can leave?"

"We don't want to rush your recovery, for it may lead to permanent damage." Hestia glanced at Phoenix's wound. It was entirely black now, and just looking at it made me shudder. "I'd say by noon you'll be good to go."

"That's quick," Phoenix noted.

Hestia shrugged. "Some of the so-called professionals that work at your hospitals have no idea what they're doing. Once I went to a hospital to meet an old friend and came across a doctor using tilly and lysdonia seeds for a nasty cut, when it clearly should've been tilly and *florant*. Honestly—amateur mistakes!"

"Um…" I raised my eyebrow.

"How is it different?" Phoenix asked, her eyes lighting up.

Was she *actually* eating this up?

Hestia peered at Phoenix with great interest. "How is *what* different?"

"Lysdonia seeds and florant? What's the difference? And how is one better for healing cuts?"

Hestia looked at Phoenix, puzzled, but launched straight into a lecture about how florant, for one, has much better texture, and has better healing ingredients, like gison and hilew, and tilly worked to clean the cut. I pretty much droned out the entire thing, focusing on Sorin, who was grazing peacefully outside.

"…While gison is good for closing things up and hilew is better for lessening the pain. Lysdonia seeds contain no gison and instead contain grolak, which stops the pain but doesn't heal the actual cut. Of course, it'd be nice if florant included grolak, but nobody's perfect, and too much would overdose the cut, or else you'd put in—"

There was suddenly a loud, rumbling sound. Embarrassed, I gave my loud stomach a miffed look and glanced back up at Hestia, who did not look happy at being interrupted.

"Did you eat any of the food I set for you?" Hestia asked.

"Not yet," I admitted.

"Bring your tray into the kitchen. Both of you can finish up your meals there," Hestia said decisively.

Two minutes later, we were sitting in a small kitchen, squished into the smallest table I'd ever seen. I could barely move my elbows without someone yelping in surprise and scowling at me.

"No... no..." Hestia muttered after a while, lost in her thoughts.

"'No... no...' what?" Phoenix asked, spooning the last bits of her mashed potatoes.

"Glavio hardly prepared you for this treacherous journey."

Tingling annoyance manifested inside me. "What do you mean he didn't *prepare* us? Didn't you see our packs? And we trained forever!"

"That is all true," Hestia gandered up at me. There was something unsettling about her, and I couldn't put my finger on it until her eyes fully changed to a light lavender. Before I could scream, Hestia continued. "Still, you need to learn to fix yourself from battle injuries."

"How would you know that?" I snapped, quickly forgetting her eyes.

"This is not the last time you will get hurt, and without mending yourself, you'd be sitting ducks." Hestia's eyes flickered. They were changing again, this time to blue. She shook her head, her eyes turning back to brown. "Don't misunderstand me. I don't blame you."

"You blame Glavio," I concluded, glaring at her.

"Yes," Hestia agreed without hesitation. "He is very wise, but this oversight was stupid."

"Are you calling Glavio—"

"Yes, I am, in this instance," Hestia interrupted calmly. "You will need a healer for your journey."

My eyes widened. "Wait. You aren't thinking—"

"Oh no, I shall not accompany you." Hestia turned to Phoenix. "I believe I can help you."

And when I let out a huge, relieved sigh, all eyes turned to me, Hestia's in particular more scary than the others, because hers were changing to a dark, stormy grey.

***

I'm not exactly sure how Hestia 'helped' Phoenix, because right after the conversation, Hestia rushed us up to bed, and the next morning, I overslept. When I came down for breakfast, Phoenix was rising from the table, an empty plate in front of her.

"You're late," Hestia greeted.

"I didn't know I was on the clock," I retorted, grabbing an apple off the table and circling to Phoenix, who was biting her lip. "Are you okay? All healed up, I mean?"

She nodded. "Feeling great, thanks to Hestia's inspiring healing."

I didn't like how she said 'inspiring.'

"Let's get going. You have a long ride ahead of you," Hestia told us, hurrying us out the door before I could respond. "Sorin and your carriage are ready for you."

"Another carriage?" I said, feeling guilty about the two we had already destroyed.

"You can't do this journey without one. So, despite your history with carriages, I have to give you one. Consider bringing it back when you are done," Hestia admonished mockingly.

We scrambled aboard, Pheonix in the back and I taking the reins.

"Oh, yes, and by the way, I told Phoenix," Hestia called, "the first Rose you seek is in Trenton."

"She has a rare copy of one section of the *Powerful Artifacts of Arma*, which deals with healing but also happens to mention one Rose," explained Phoenix through the window.

"That's where the library is too," I recognized.

"That's a good thing, too. Trenton is one of the best guarded cities in Arma. It safeguards numerous precious contents of the library. Given your mission, it will also save you some flying. Maybe it will give you fewer chances to wreck another carriage," she said playfully. Her mocking undertone rubbed me; it was as if she thought we were on a fool's errand and destined to fail. Was I being too sensitive? I understood that my dislike of Hestia was unreasonable. She had been nothing but helpful. Yet, I couldn't help myself.

I turned my attention to the sky and flicked the reins. Sorin whinnied loudly, as if saying *It's about time!* and galloped into take-off. The familiar lurching feeling in my stomach emerged as we ascended farther from the ground. Soon, we were in the crisp, cold, air, with clouds floating beside us and Hestia's house becoming a speck on the ground.

# ELEVEN

**Personally, I'd already had enough** adventure for a lifetime, but the clear image of Glavio kept me from landing the carriage in a safe place, far away from Trenton. His pleading eyes bore into me. I told myself over and over again that we were doing this journey for him, because Glavio was worth it.

And I needed to help the wizards and sorceresses across Arma.

I *had* to.

I wasn't sure what was driving Phoenix, though. Whenever we took breaks from the air, Phoenix was always pouring over a small pocketbook Hestia had given her. We barely talked when we stopped for food. The only words spoken were Phoenix's occasional mutterings, which usually made little sense.

"Lysdonia petals and florant… no, that would backfire…"

When I asked her what she meant, she'd look up at me, startled, and say, "Huh? Oh, I'm just reading." She said it like that explained everything. After two stops, I learned it was better to just leave her alone.

Soon, Trenton glimmered below us. The city was nowhere near as dignified and beautiful as Silenia, but it was not long before we found out exactly what Hestia meant by well-guarded when we tried to enter the city limits.

Two burly looking guards, in heavy armor and swords by their side, flew at us on two burly looking pegasi with surprising speed. Before I could understand what was happening or even clearly identify the color of their eyes, two incredibly sharp swords were pointed at my throat.

My heart pounded thunderously, and my breaths sounded like hurricanes.

*What's going on? And where's Phoenix?*

I glanced nervously at the two guards. They didn't move a muscle, so I figured it was up to me to start the conversation and not get stabbed in the throat.

"Um, hi," I tried, offering a tight smile. My voice shook with each syllable. They responded by pressing their extremely sharp swords against my skin. I gulped. "Those swords of yours look *reeeeaaaaally* nice. You know what'd be even nicer? If I could admire them from a farther vantage point."

"Not likely," the guard on the left grumbled.

I let out a hollow laugh. "Look, I'm gonna call you Lefty, and you Righty, alright?" I didn't wait for an answer. "So, um, I'm trying to save the world here with my friend Phoenix. This prophecy sort of led us to Trenton. Maybe you can help us out a little?"

No answer.

"Not very talkative, eh?" I asked, a million options flying through my mind. I wanted to glance back to see if Phoenix had noticed anything, but if I did, my head would probably be watching the proceedings from the floor of the carriage, detached from my body. "Guys, WAD has sent us on this mission. You really need to give us a little room here."

"WAD?" Righty asked. "The Wizarding Agency of Defense?"

"Don't you dare," Lefty warned. "They're probably spies. Why else would they be approaching a forbidden sector?"

Forbidden?

Whoops.

"Have you got any sort of identification?" Righty asked.

"Uh…" I was getting more nervous, and Phoenix was completely oblivious of this situation, safely tucked inside the carriage. "No, but since when do you need identification to enter Trenton?" Why had Glavio not helped us with making at least the official passage easier for us? We had enough trouble from our enemies without people supposedly on our side creating more obstacles. WAD sure could have sent an advance notification about us. Was Hestia right about Glavio being too casual and sending us into a mortal mission without adequate preparation?

"We've been tipped off that there might be an attack on city boundaries," Lefty growled. "No identification, no passage."

"You two!" a man shouted. He was boxy, held a rather stern face, and rode on a rather stern-faced pegasus. "What do you think you're doing? Don't you know who these two are?" The man shook his head at me once he was next to us. "I'm sorry, you may pass. WAD has sent an advanced notification of your arrival." Okay. Not too casual. Just bureaucracy.

"Oh… thanks," I said, cooling my racing breath as the guards sheathed their swords.

I flicked the reins, ordering Sorin to fly past them. I turned around to look through the carriage window, and there was Phoenix, deeply engrossed in Hestia's pocketbook, unaware that anything out of the ordinary had occurred. I groaned with exasperation.

"Phoenix," I grumbled while searching the ground for a good landing spot. It wasn't long before we came across a public park in the middle of the big city. I pulled Sorin's reins and urged him to land in the middle of the park.

Phoenix didn't even put the book down when we were going to the ground faster than we'd ever flown before.

As soon as we landed in the middle of a large clearing with pine trees surrounding us, I climbed out of the driver's seat and threw open the carriage door. Phoenix was still pouring over her book.

"Phoenix," I growled.

Phoenix looked up and scrunched her nose. "What's up with you?"

"What's... what's up with *me?*" I sputtered. "You want to know what's up with me? Maybe the fact that you're more interested in that stupid book than our quest! Did you even realize that two city guards nearly took my head off?"

Phoenix narrowed her eyes. "I was reading, Seamus."

"Yeah, I noticed!"

"Do you not want me to read?"

"Not when I have two swords pointed at my throat!"

Phoenix gaped at me, unsure whether I was telling the truth or not. "Was that a metaphor or—"

*"It wasn't a metaphor! Didn't you notice we stopped in the air for fifteen minutes?"*

"I was absorbed in the book—"

"Two guards stopped us and pointed swords at my throat! If you stopped reading, you could've helped!"

"I—"

I continued to interrupt her angrily. "There's a reason the prophecy mentioned *both of us*. Because both of us are supposed to be on this quest! One of us right now is just a tourist."

"Well, why do you think I'm reading, if it isn't for our quest?"

"It'd be helpful to figure that out if I *knew* what you were reading, because every time I ask you, all you say is, 'Oh, I'm just reading!'"

"It's a book about *healing*! That's what Hestia meant when she said Glavio hadn't sent us on our quest prepared. That's what she meant when she said we'd need a healer on our quest. She recognized my interest in healing and told me it was an opportunity too good to pass up, so she gave me this book. I've been trying to learn about healing ever since, so maybe we won't need to shout '*Alenia*' every time we get in trouble!"

"Actually, '*Alenia*' only works once—"

"Even more of a reason that I learn some healing."

I sighed. "Okay, fine, I get it." I gazed down at the grass.

Phoenix took a deep breath to calm herself. "I'm sorry. I could have explained earlier. "

"Now we really need to focus on getting the first Rose," I declared, my nerves lurching inside me, the words all too real for my own comfort. "Assuming Calypso doesn't already have it," I added.

"She couldn't possibly know where it is," Phoenix said. "Glavio said the only thing that knows the location of the Roses is the secret book."

"That's assuming Calypso hasn't found another way to get to the Roses or hasn't found the book first. Hestia told us the first Rose was in Trenton, and she can't be the only one who knows. Calypso's got a lot of people on her side."

"True, but Hestia is not just another person."

Ugh. Her admiration for Hestia…

I had to force myself to not respond testily. "Fine. Right now, we need to focus on finding the first Rose." I glanced around. "How are we supposed to find an all-powerful Rose in the middle of Trenton? I'm guessing if we ask around, we're not going to get our answer."

Phoenix didn't reply, but instead closed her eyes and hummed. I waited for her to open her eyes and help me figure this out, but when she stayed like that for a minute, I began to get impatient.

"What in the world are you—"

Phoenix's eyes lit up as soon as she opened them. "Really, Seamus, healing isn't the only thing Hestia taught me." She squinted in the opposite direction, like she was searching for something. "The Roses leave a trail of power behind them."

I frowned. "I don't feel anything."

"You can't just feel them. Hestia taught me how to search for the trail of power."

My mouth went dry. "So… wouldn't Calypso know this too?"

"There is no point thinking about that. Let's just focus on what we can control." Did Hestia transform my friend to Phoenix-the-Zen in one night? She was not wrong though.

"Alright, fine," I agreed stiffly, running my hand through my hair impatiently. "Hopefully, she was busy doing something else, maybe tracking us down."

"Is that supposed to be the bright side?"

"You wanna give it a go?"

Phoenix closed her eyes again, and this time her humming grew louder and stronger. She opened her eyes and gazed at me intensely. Her breath caught.

"I know where it is." Phoenix murmured. "Follow me…"

We trudged through Trenton, animated, Phoenix leading Sorin behind me. We passed ice-cream shops, bakeries, and delicious-smelling restaurants that had all kinds of tasty food. My stomach growled. Phoenix heard too because she looked back with a raised eyebrow.

"What? It's been hours since we ate at Hestia's."

"Hurry up," ordered Phoenix, ignoring my comment.

But something nailed to a restaurant caught my eye.

"Wait... Phoenix... look at this..."

Frowning, Phoenix turned and squinted at where I was pointing. At the top it read *'Missing,'* and underneath that in big letters *'Eliza, WAD agent,'* and underneath that a picture of Eliza, which had an unmistakable resemblance to the chief we had met at WAD headquarters.

*Missing?*

A pit in my stomach grew deeper. Glavio suspended. Elizia missing. What was happening at WAD?

Phoenix grabbed my hand. "I... I don't know, Seamus," she stuttered. "But we have to keep going..." Her voice trailed off, clearly not liking this new information either.

I shook my head, but Phoenix began trekking across the street once again. With one last piercing glance at the 'Missing' poster, I turned and followed.

It wasn't long before we had left the city behind us, its lights twinkling in the distance. In front of us was a large, beautiful lake that basked and shimmered in the setting sun's light. The thick wood near the lake swayed in the breeze. It was a perfect evening.

Unbeknownst to me, it was about to be ruined big time.

"We should hurry," I warned, eyeing the sunset. "I'm pretty sure retrieving the Rose before dark would be better."

"*That* I agree with."

"So, where's the trail leading us" I asked.

Phoenix frowned and turned to the left. Almost instantaneously, all the color drained from her face. Her knees wobbled.

"Phoenix..." I started anxiously, getting a serious wave of déjà vu. "*What's wrong?*" I breathed.

"Seamus—" she started, her eyes fixed behind me.

"*What is it?*" I hissed, fear swirling inside me.

Phoenix swallowed the tiniest gulp. "Look." She pointed behind me, over the trees and across the deserted roads.

I inhaled sharply.

Looming over everything and casting shadows so big I was sure I was dreaming, was a large, ancient-looking colosseum. The crumbling site lay in ruins, and in the middle of it were three large pillars, all with gargoyles standing stiff on top of them with angry, miffed looks frozen on their faces. In the middle of the pillars was one, imposing stone tower—but that wasn't the scary part.

There, perched on top of it, was an enormous bird with razor-sharp claws and piercing eyes, batting its wings and searching for food.

"Hide!" Phoenix hissed, and both of us ducked behind a bush. Sorin casually grazed behind us, unaware of a monstrous bird searching the ground.

"What is that thing?" I whispered, unable to take my eyes off the huge bird as it let out a bone-rattling screech and devoured an entire flock of pigeons.

"It looks like a roc," Phoenix hissed. "Huge predators that feast upon travelers. It's said that they can devour elephants whole. This one probably has a nest up there, which is really bad news. Rocs are super protective of their eggs until they hatch. If we get anywhere close to that tower, she'll dive down and eat us for dinner."

"So, what do we do?"

Phoenix studied the ruins. "Of course… The colosseum is in ruins, but the pillars and towers are in perfect condition. It only makes sense. Three pillars—the three Pillars of Arma. And a roc just happens to have a nest up there? That bird was put there on purpose. This has to be where the first Rose is."

"Now that we've confirmed that—we still have a monster bird at the top of the tower. How are we supposed to get past a *roc*?"

"I've got an idea," Phoenix said suddenly, squinting at the roc. "I'll distract her since I'm faster," I cringed, "and you kill her."

"*Kill* her? Isn't that a bit… callous?" I asked uncertainly, gazing at Phoenix, who was flipping through her book hastily. "I mean, she does have eggs and all, so—"

"Do you know what mother rocs do to their babies once they're fully grown?" Phoenix snapped, glancing up. "Either they eat them or leave them alone to fend for themselves."

"They *eat* their babies?" I felt sick.

"Usually. That's the only reason they're protective of them, because they don't enjoy giving up a good meal."

I didn't say anything.

"*And* we need to save the Roses. Remember, Glavio's counting on us. So is all of WAD. Plus, all the other wizards and witches that live in Arma. Oh, yeah, don't you forget that if we don't do this, Arma will be weakened bit by bit until Calypso can fully take over?"

Even though I hated to say it, Phoenix had a good point. If we didn't get the Rose, wizarding magic as we knew it would be over, and Arma would be 'weakened bit by bit' until Calypso—or her master—ended it once and for all.

I wasn't going to give up that easily.

"You've made your point." I exhaled. "How do we kill it?"

Phoenix came up quickly with a plan. "I'll run across the court and get her to attack me," Phoenix decided. "As it swoops down towards me, you move in from behind and take it by surprise. Make sure it's dead. If you leave it injured but still alive, there's no way we'd survive."

I nodded, summoning confidence from every forgotten corner of me. I remembered what Glavio told me and swallowed. "Do it, Phoenix. Just, please… be careful, okay?"

"I will." Phoenix looked at me, her eyes an endless ocean, and sucked in a deep breath. "This is probably the craziest thing I've ever done in my life, but… here we go." She jumped up and lit her hands on fire. Then she broke into a run, as fast as she could, towards the roc, sparking flames like a jet across the courtyard.

I dashed to the other side of the tower, where I could get a good shot from behind. Where would her weak spot be? The pressure threatened to squeeze me to pieces as I tried to recall Glavio's words.

*A natural weak spot of all animals is their underbelly. That is where most hunters aim for. It will bring your enemy down easily.*

How was I going to get under it without it noticing me?

Phoenix tore across the fields, aflame with fire. Bright orange shot out from under her. A huge column of flames burst from her arms. That got the roc's attention. Its sharp eyes fixated on Phoenix, who was now yelling and jumping up and down. I didn't take the deadly look it was giving her as a good sign, and next thing I knew, the roc swooped down into an elegant dive, its yellow eyes glaring at Phoenix's flames.

I bolted after it, watching the fight as it went on. The roc roared, clacking its beak at Phoenix fiercely, but it couldn't get close enough to the flames without catching fire itself.

I wasn't sure how much longer Phoenix could hold an entire flame engulfing her since it's physically pretty demanding, and I didn't want to take any chances. I plunged at the roc, my heart racing, and slid underneath it, Alexander's sword growing in my hands. I was just about to stab it, when it hurled upwards, finally giving up on Phoenix.

That's when it caught sight of me, and even from up there, I'm pretty sure my sword didn't give it any good ideas.

It dove at me with a speed so astonishing that I wasn't sure whether she was falling or flying. A terrified look cemented on Phoenix's face.

*The flames protecting her were gone.*

"Now might be a good time to run," I whispered, my eyes fixed on the humongous predator quacking its beak, ready for a free meal.

"RUN!" Phoenix screamed, snapping us back to our senses.

We spun around and scampered in the other direction.

I chanced a glance over my shoulder, and my eyes widened. The roc was speeding towards us, flexing her sharp, glinting claws.

"Split up!" I hollered. "And engulf yourself in fire!"

"You go left, I go right!" Phoenix commanded. With the roc gaining on us, we split in separate directions.

After her experience with Phoenix's flames, the roc decided I'd be the better target. But since not everyone could surround themselves in fire whenever they wanted, I was completely defenseless, except for Alexander's sword and my power—though I wasn't sure how I could defend myself with just my blade and some water.

The roc gained on me with alarming speed, her claws extended. Phoenix bounded at us with her dagger in her hand, but I knew there was no way she'd make it in time.

That's when I did the stupidest thing ever.

I turned around and shouted, "Come and get me, you oversized birdbrain!"

The roc roared furiously and sped at me like a bullet, so powerful that when it passed, trees uprooted from their spots and flung through the air like pebbles. Terror froze my bones. *Why the heck did I do that?* I asked my idiot self.

Before it could smash into me, I dove out of the way and slashed at its claws. Luckily, I rolled out of the way. Unfortunately, roc claws are super tough, and my attempted slash probably felt like a paper cut—painful but definitely non-lethal.

The roc turned around and dove towards me. I held my sword above my head and slid under her, slashing at her feathery underbelly as she passed. The roc bellowed in agony, halting in midair. If it's possible for a roc to look furious, humiliated, and deadly at the same time, that's what she looked like.

She flew at me with a petrifying speed, considering the nasty cut I had given her. Her feathers ruffled in the wind, and her eyes were dreadful and infuriated. Her underbelly was now glazed red. I held my sword up, ready to fight when she came again. But before I could do anything, her claws extended out, and too late, I realized what she was going to do.

The roc seized my sword with her claws and sped towards the trees, unclasping it far away from me. I watched it plunge into the reaching trees and stick straight into the ground in dismay.

So, she wasn't a complete birdbrain.

She circled in the air, facing me.

My eyes sped, ignoring the pounding of my heart and the struggle to breath, between her coming at me with the speed of a flying cheetah and Alexander's sword, which lay too far to get to.

There was no way to defend myself.

This was it. That face was going to be the last thing I ever saw. The feathered face of a gigantic bird.

She was so close… I was so close to death… Stone, cold death…

Something silver streaked through the sky and stabbed the roc straight in its side. The roc's eyes went wide, and it roared angrily.

There was Phoenix, standing defiantly behind it.

Good news: I was still alive! Bad news: The roc was, too, and it was angrier than before. It swooped down at me, ignoring Phoenix, who just burst into flames.

Out of the corner of my eye, I watched Phoenix grab my sword and catapult it at me as fast as possible. I dove out of the way before the roc could tear me to pieces, leaping up and snatching my sword out of the air. The roc fixed its eyes on me.

I tightened my grip on the sword, leapt towards the roc, and flew at it with my sword above my head and a Tarzan yell hurtling out of my mouth. For a moment, time slowed down, and all I could see was the roc's feathers. But then it sped up again. I stabbed the roc with all my might, using the last of my strength and rolling on to the grass.

With a pained screech, the roc plummeted towards the ground, which shook the dry earth around her.

I landed not far from the roc, my feet aching from the force of the fall.

Phoenix raced towards me and slid down beside me, concern outlining her face. "Seamus, are you okay?"

"Yeah." I sucked in a breath and smiled weakly at her. "Thanks for the save, though. Without that dagger, I'd probably be roc meat."

"What are best friends for?"

I wiped the sweat off my forehead.

Before I could respond, howling reverberated through the nearby woods. My head snapped up, and my eyes focused on the trees. It was complete silence for a moment, but then sounds came again: a howl, and then whining barks.

"No," Phoenix whispered.

A loud, strident sound echoed in my ears, and scores of wolves appeared out of the woods and many more from the other side of the ruins, surrounding us. They had demon eyes and wickedly sharp claws.

"We defeated that roc for Calypso!" Phoenix thundered, realization sweeping over her. "She *used* us! She was waiting in the woods for one of us to finish the other so that she can take on the exhausted survivor."

Red anger blurred my vision, and each breath seemed trapped inside me as I struggled to understand.

*For Calypso. For Calypso. For Calypso.*

Animosity tore through me, and I tightened my grip on my sword furiously. Spit flew from my mouth as I roared before I could stop myself, "SHOW YOURSELF, CALYPSO!"

# TWELVE

**Wolves from all** sides advanced hungrily on us, and all I could think about was that we had just killed a roc, and we couldn't get a break? With our luck, a thunderbird would appear right next to the wolves screaming, *Bring it on, losers!*

Then I noticed something weird about the wolves' teeth. I nudged Phoenix and pointed.

"Do you see that?" I whispered.

"What do you want me to see? An army of wolves surrounding us that is about to tear us apart?" she hissed back.

"Their slobber—it's *yellow.*"

"Yellow?" She squinted at the wolves who were advancing on us, getting closer and closer, inch by inch.

Her eyes widened. "Seamus, this is bad. Really, really bad. Do you know what that means?"

"Calypso is gross?"

Phoenix gave me a dirty look. "They aren't any regular wolves. Their bites are *poisonous*. If one of those wolves even manages to break our skin, we'll probably die."

"Comforting." I fixed my eyes on one particular wolf advancing slowly. "So don't let them even touch us. Thanks."

"Seamus…" Phoenix's voice trailed off.

I glanced up, frowning. "What's—" I stopped mid-sentence, my eyes stuck on the wolves. They stopped inching towards us and growled threateningly, their red eyes boring through us as they hunched their shoulders like they were getting ready to pounce.

"That's not good."

Phoenix began whispering fast. "As soon as I say so, you climb up the tower as fast as you can, get the Rose, and then get out of here."

"*Without* you? Phoenix, there's no way I'm leaving—"

"If you don't leave me, then we're both toast." She turned to look at me, just the slightest glance, and fear and desperation cascaded in her eyes. My hands balled into fists.

"I don't care. I'm not leaving you."

"If you don't leave me, every Armanian's life is ruined! Calypso wins, and all the other wizards out there don't deserve that!"

"*You* don't deserve this!"

The wolves were getting antsy. They were going to jump any minute. We didn't have much time.

"It doesn't matter!" Phoenix grasped my hand. My eyes stung as I glared at her, but she kept her eyes on the wolves. "I——" She stopped, then pushed me away. "Go. You have to go."

"Phoenix——"

"Think about Arma, Seamus! *Please!*"

I watched Phoenix's determined eyes with fear and uncertainty. "I'll come back for you," I promised, wishing my dry throat would clear and my stuck eyes would look away.

Emptiness numbed my chest into a bottomless hole that could never be filled.

Before Phoenix could respond, the wolves decided they were done waiting. The first one launched itself at Phoenix, and she slashed at its chest instinctively, unharmed. Her eyes closed as three more menacing wolves leapt into the air. A wall of fire burst up from the ground and caught the wolves that launched themselves at us, causing them to scamper away whining, but there were still the others, growling at the fire with hunger in their eyes.

"GO!" Phoenix screamed. "I've never been able to hold a wall of fire longer than five minutes!"

Without a second thought, I dashed to the tower and contemplated my chances. Loose bricks poked out of it not too far apart. I seized the first block and began climbing up. A tiny glance down, and I thrust my head up, my fingers shaking with fear. I gulped. One slip, and I'd be wolf meat.

Phoenix's wall of fire faltered. A large wolf lunged at me. I yelped and lost hold on one of my hands, swinging to the side while attempting to reach for my sword. The wolf missed, just barely.

"Focus!" Phoenix howled, sweat steaming off her as she managed to get the fire wall up again. "Just get the Rose!"

I managed to swing to the side again, slamming against the cold tower. I grasped another loose brick and forced my sore legs to climb, willing myself not to squeeze my eyes shut and stay paralyzed in one spot.

I climbed as fast as I could, my muscles screaming for a rest and my legs close to giving away.

*Come on, come on!*

*Let me live, please… please… let me live…* I prayed.

The top of the tower was only a few more bricks away. I peeked down a tiny bit and immediately jolted my head back up, my eyes wide. The ground looked *miles* below me.

Reminding myself I didn't have much time before Phoenix's wall of fire broke and the pack of wolves attacked, I reached for the next brick. I had to get back to her before that happened... somehow.

I climbed higher and higher before, finally, I managed to pull myself up onto the top of the tower. I lay there for a second, letting my limbs recover a bit. Part of me wanted to drift off to sleep then and there, but I forced myself to my feet and flashed my eyes down at Phoenix's faint figure, who was down on her knees. I gritted my teeth.

My moment of relief was over. I needed to get the Rose.

If I didn't...

Not gonna go there.

*"Please... please... please..."* I prayed, my eyes squeezed shut as I circled around. A sigh escaped me, whether from awe or relief, I wasn't sure. There was the Rose, glowing with power, floating an inch above a stump made of stones. It had crystal petals that shone with light and a long, gracious golden stem with golden leaves reaching from it.

Starstruck, I stood there for a moment, gazing at it, before jerking myself back to my senses. I rushed to the stump and carefully took the Rose from its place, diminishing its magical glow, and gingerly placed it in my backpack. Then I scampered to the edge of the tower, ignoring my pounding heart as I frowned down, my eyes narrowing.

Then the worst thing in the world hit me.

I needed to climb *down*!

Flickering in the corner of my eye distracted me from the frightening sight. More terror. I whipped my head around to find the wall of fire weakening. Panic built up inside me, and ideas flew through my head, each more desperate than the last. If Phoenix's barrier broke, we were both dead. Because there was no way I was going to leave Phoenix down there and try to escape. One thing for sure, I needed to get both of us out of here alive. But how?

My eyebrows creased as I squinted into the sky, trying to make out something that rocketed towards me. It had furrowed wings and shot towards me like a brown bullet.

Realization gusted over me. *"SORIN!"* I bellowed, grinning and waving my arms wildly. "SORIN, OVER HERE!"

The brown bullet launched itself at me. I dove out of the way with panic as it crashed on to the tower roof. Shielding my face, I slowly rose to my feet. Sorin stood up shakily, but the look on his face was nothing but pride. I grinned widely, patting him quickly.

"You're *amazing*, Sorin, you know that?"

Sorin whinnied, as if agreeing with me, and spread his wings. I clambered onto his back and pointed at Phoenix, who looked like she was about to surrender. How long had I been climbing for? Four minutes? We didn't have much time.

"Hyah!" I shouted, and Sorin took off through the hole. I led him down to Phoenix as the wall flickered on and off for a second, then disappeared.

*"PHOENIX!"* I shouted, holding out my hand.

She galloped towards me as wolves lunged at her. I leaned down so far, I was sure I was going to fall, and I reached for her arm desperately. Closing my eyes, I felt my fingers grasp her arms as we took off into the sky. My eyes flew open as I tightened my grip on her arm resolutely. The wolves sprang at her, missing her by inches.

"Seamus…" Phoenix's eyes looked like they were about to glaze over. They were glassy and grey instead of amber. "Thank you."

"You need arius," I said urgently, gripping her arm, "just until we can get you to a real doctor." I pulled her up onto Sorin shakily. She leaned on me, breathing softly. "You'll be okay, Phoenix," I promised quietly.

She had to be.

But we didn't have enough time. We didn't have enough time to find a healer, and we needed one *right now*.

I seized a pack of arius out of my pocket and fed her spoons of it, my fingers white. The color slowly began to return to her face, but her eyes were still glassy and grey, and her face was still pale.

"Oh, no… *Phoenix*, just stay with me for a little longer, okay?" I begged, feeding her another spoon of arius. That was a bit dangerous, but I was out of ideas. My eyes fell on a pocketbook peeking out of Phoenix's pocket.

*Stupid Hestia.*

But it was my best shot.

"Sorin, land us down there," I ordered, pointing at a grassy field that reminded me of the one I used to practice sword fighting with Glavio. "Be gentle."

Sorin softly landed us in the field, and held out his wings so we could slide off. I helped Phoenix off, but as soon as her feet hit the ground, she collapsed.

I gasped and Sorin neighed with fear. I dove down and grabbed her pocketbook, flipping through it frantically. Finally, I found one for regaining strength. There was writing scrawled at the bottom of the page.

Lysdonia seeds are a good choice because they contain grolak, which Hestia told me lessens the pain. But it's not just pain someone is dealing with when they collapse from overuse of powers, it is also dangerously low levels of basic life elements. If the condition persists for too long, it can be fatal. Rozberries are required to shore up the life elements. Mash up rozberries and lysdonia seeds along with a bit of pure water and then eat the paste. This should help regain strength.

I bit my lip. Should I trust Phoenix, who had just learned healing a day ago, to save her own life?

*But this is based on what Hestia taught her, and as much as I hate to admit it, she is a good healer.*

There was no time to waste. I turned to Sorin. "Stay here and make sure Phoenix is okay. I'm going to find something to help her."

Sorin neighed in promise.

I whirled around and took off towards the forest, which was not too far away. Lysdonia seeds would be found on the outskirts of it, while rozberries would be found in the bushes. If I was lucky, I wouldn't have to go too far into the forest.

As soon as I reached the forest, I tore at flowers and scoured bushes. It wasn't long before I spotted a huge lysdonia flower towering over the other flowers.

I shot at it and jumped up, grabbing a petal and pulling it down. How many lysdonia seeds would I need? I didn't have time to figure it out. I plucked the entire flower and thought of putting it in my backpack, but remembered the Rose, so I held tightly on to it and raced through the forest, searching for the slightest shade of red.

Finally, after what felt like hours, I nearly rammed straight into a rozberry bush. I picked as many as I could and bolted back to Sorin and Phoenix.

As soon as I reached them, I clutched the flower head and pulled the lysdonia as hard as I could. I rubbed the head against my hand, and its seeds rained down. I took all of them, and having no better idea, mashed them up with the rozberries in my hands. Soon, the mash was complete, and I closed my eyes, summoning the water inside of me and morphing it into a ball to place the mash inside it. It is very hard to hold everything together, but desperate times call on unknown strength. I twirled the water ball around in the air to mix them up and floated it towards Phoenix.

"Phoenix," I whispered, "eat this."

Phoenix's eyes were barely open. She nodded so slightly that I wasn't sure if she even saw it. Then she opened her mouth a bit, and I gave her the mash.

It took her a while to swallow it. For a minute, nothing happened, and I just waited there, praying.

Then it happened. Color returned to her face, and her eyes opened a little and were no longer so glassy. I stayed by her side the entire time, feeding Sorin carrots and telling him what an amazing pegasus he was. It wasn't long before Sorin fell asleep, but seeing Phoenix passed out, I just couldn't let my body relax.

Hour after hour I waited. Darkness soon took over us, but I didn't want to risk moving Phoenix to the carriage.

Finally, Phoenix's eyes fluttered open, and she slowly sat up. "Seamus… Seamus, what happened?" Her eyes widened. "Oh, no! We lost, didn't we?"

I almost laughed out loud with relief as I pulled her in for a hug. "I was so worried, Phoenix. You were knocked out for so long..." Then I pulled away and surveyed Phoenix. "How do you feel? What's the last thing you remember?"

"The wall of fire... and then, the pegasus ride... Did you get the Rose?" Phoenix asked, alarmed.

"Calm down. You missed a few hours," I told her, setting her back down on the grass. "I got the Rose from the top of the tower."

"Really? That's amazing!" Phoenix beamed with triumph. Then she looked sideways at my backpack. "We need to get it somewhere safe."

"Right now, we need to find somewhere for you to regain your strength. We'll worry more about the Rose tomorrow. There are plenty of inns around here."

"Okay," Phoenix agreed. "We can walk—"

"No," I said firmly as Phoenix tried to stand up, but fell back on her hands and rubbed her head, a pained expression on her face. "You'll ride on Sorin. I'll walk."

Phoenix smiled weakly. "Thank you."

Fifteen minutes later, we managed to check into an inn. Phoenix snored on one of the beds, and I stared at the ceiling, struggling to count sheep, but every time the sheep hopped away and disappeared, I immediately thought of the Rose going poof and glanced under the bed where we had cleverly hidden it. It was hard to make it fit in—with its glow, crystal petals, and golden stem—but we figured it out in the end.

It took at least two hours, but finally the ceiling disappeared, and I sunk into a deep sleep.

# THIRTEEN

**"Joining me would've been the** best choice, Seamus…" a voice hissed. I whirled around, only able to see darkness. When I tried to cry out, to ask who was there, my voice wouldn't work.

"The deal is still on the table," whispered the voice. It seemed to be coming from all around me, like it was talking to me while spinning around in a tornado.

"You could still join me, boy… It would be the best option… Much better than risking your life day and night…"

Suddenly, my voice worked again, and I shouted, "Calypso? What are you, too much of a coward to show yourself?"

"Oh, I am not Calypso…" hissed the voice. "I am much more *powerful*… I am her master…"

"Her master?" I asked, turning as the voice shifted.

"Join me…" was all the voice said, its ringing getting louder in my ears. *"Join me, Seamus!"*

I jolted straight up in bed, sweating. Sunlight shone through the window, and I spotted Phoenix busy at the stove. I raised my eyebrows. Was Phoenix *cooking*?

"Breakfast?" I asked, trying to shake off the horrible feeling of ice trickling down my spine.

Phoenix turned around and grinned at me. "You're up! And, yes, I bought breakfast from downstairs. I'm just heating up the eggs and pancakes for us. Are you hungry?"

"Starving," I answered, climbing out of bed and grabbing clothes to take into the bathroom and change. "How are you feeling?"

"I'm alright," Phoenix answered, flipping a pancake masterfully on to a plate, with scrambled eggs served next to it. She peered up at me as I emerged from the bathroom and frowned. "Why are you sweating?"

"No reason," I muttered. "Just hungry."

"Pretty sure you don't sweat when you're hungry."

I sighed, wishing, as I had many times before, that Phoenix was less pushy. "It's nothing, really. I just dreamt of a really creepy voice that was supposedly Calypso's master, and it told me I should've joined him instead of risking my life day and night." I laughed weakly at the expression on Phoenix's face. "It was scarier when it happened."

"Calypso's *master*?" Phoenix asked, setting the plate of pancake and eggs down on the table. "Glavio said she wasn't working alone. What did he sound like? Where were you in the dream? What did he look like?"

"I didn't actually see him," I told her, recalling the details of the dream. "I wasn't anywhere, either. I was just standing in the middle of the dark. And his voice came from many different places every time he spoke, like he was moving around. It felt like I was in a hurricane of shadows."

Phoenix huffed a breath. "That doesn't tell us *anything*," she complained in a frustrated tone. "We still don't know who Calypso's master is, and we *still* don't have *Powerful Artifacts of Arma*!"

"We'll go searching for it today," I promised as I dove into the pancake. "Do we have a self-refilling whipped cream bottle around here?"

She shot me a look, and I shut myself up.

"Okay, so *Powerful Artifacts of Arma* is in Trenton, where we are right now," Phoenix said, unrolling a map of Arma on the table. On the map, Leon was circled in faded ink. It seemed like forever ago that I had wanted to travel to the Bridge city, to be in the midst of all the chaos. Phoenix circled Trenton in bolder ink as she said, "The first Rose has been found." She check marked Trenton.

"Now we just need to find the other two Roses, and to do that, we need to find that book." She turned to me. "Largest library in Arma—haven't you been here before?"

I nodded. "Glavio was talking about the St. Henderson Library. It's ancient—people go there to tour it, but hardly ever check out any books. Do you think it'd be under section *P* in the historical part, or under the author's name?"

Phoenix rolled her eyes. "You and your sense of humor that you wish were funny."

"Hey, my sense of humor *is* funny!" I protested.

She grinned. "It will not be at an obvious place. Maybe, it'll be hidden cleverly in one of the books or bookshelves. Speaking of which," she gestured to under the bed, where the Rose was hidden, "when we take that with us, we'll have to be super careful to make sure no one sees it."

"It's going to be in my backpack. Who's going to see it?"

"Just don't be irresponsible, like you always are."

I shook my head, exasperated. Once, my parents bought me a turtle, and I accidentally starved it. He lasted for almost a week before I found him in his tank, dead.

"Forget about Dribble for a second, will you? He lived a good life. He was an old turtle when he came to live with me, anyway."

Phoenix shook her head. "He didn't last a week."

"Oh, forget about Dribble!" I stood up, snatching a pancake off my plate and stuffing it in my mouth. Then I mumbled with my mouth full, "We're trying to save the world, and you're still thinking about Dribble?"

"You were crying when you dug a grave for him," Phoenix teased.

"He was a good turtle, and I was six," I grumbled hotly, reaching under the bed and seizing my backpack, which held the Rose in it. "Now, do you want to keep standing around and wasting time over my long gone Dribble—" I stopped for a second, feeling sad, "or do you want to save the world and find the Roses of Arma?"

Phoenix took the backpack from me. "We need to get to the second Rose before Calypso does. Do you know when the library opens?"

"Probably in ten minutes," I answered, scanning my watch, which read seven fifty. "Let's pick up Sorin on the way—he's still downstairs in the barn."

Phoenix was already at the door. She tossed me the backpack, and I caught it, glaring.

"That has an extremely delicate ancient artifact," I chided.

Phoenix shook her head. "Don't let anyone see it," she warned and turned to head out.

***

The St. Henderson Library was *huge*, nearly as big as the line that piled outside of it. It was made with white marble that gleamed in the morning sunlight. Its windows were glassy and had strange patterns on them that depicted things like good and evil, and in the middle of it all was a window with a picture of an open book, like it was telling a story. On the side of the library was the biggest window—it was what looked like a woman with angel wings. She had her hair in a bun and had slight wrinkles. Her eyes were kind and blue. She wore a flowing white dress that fluttered majestically behind her. In her hand she carried a book like it was a baby, looking fondly down at it.

In other words, the St. Henderson library looked more like a *museum* than a library.

Still, being the biggest library in the world is no easy feat. And, neither is the line of visitors. It started at the door and snaked around the block.

I didn't even understand how there was a *line* at the library. Was there a limit to how many people could go in or something?

"There's no way we have time to wait in that line," I told Phoenix as we parked outside the library with our carriage. "We'll have to sneak in somehow."

"Let's go around," Phoenix suggested as she slid out of the back of the carriage. "There's probably a backdoor or something, and if not, we can break through one of these windows." She grinned.

Phoenix fastened Sorin's lead to a tree branch, and I followed her behind the library. The back wasn't much different than the front; it just didn't have a line looping out of its doors.

"There!" Phoenix whispered, pointing at a truck where men were unloading boxes—that were most assuredly full of books—into the library through wide open doors. "We need to sneak inside and start searching." She turned to look at me carefully. "Please, Seamus, don't be as clumsy as you usually are."

I stared at her, aghast. "*Me? Clumsy?*"

She waved her hand at me and squinted at the men taking the boxes out and putting them in the library dock. "How are we going to get in? Hide in one of the boxes?"

I snorted, and ignoring the look she was giving me, searched the truck for another option. Suddenly, an idea struck.

Oblivious to the awesomeness of my idea, Phoenix complained, "Why couldn't WAD just tell everybody about the Roses and how we're looking for them?"

Ignoring her complaint, I clutched a large rock in my hand and hurled it as hard as I could at the truck. The rock hit the truck with a loud thud, and every single one of the men looked up, frowning at the rock.

"Who did that?" yelled the man closest to the spot the rock hit.

Then I swooped down and clutched a smaller rock, throwing it silently in the other direction. The men glared in the direction the rock had been flung. "Who's there?" shouted the same man. He glanced back at the other men. "Stay here and keep working. This is ridiculous."

Then he trotted off to search for the source of hurtling rocks.

Okay, so maybe my idea wasn't as brilliant as I thought. It only got rid of one person, which really didn't help us.

"Well, that worked *splendidly*," complimented Phoenix. "Any other bright ideas? We're wasting time."

"Well, at least I got rid of *one* of them," I retorted. Then I glanced at the men and looked at us. That's when I *actually* came up with a brilliant idea.

"Phoenix," I whispered quietly, "I need you to engulf yourself in fire, okay? Leave the rest to me."

She frowned at me as I crouched down in a ready position and prepared to jump out of the bush. "Three, two, one—" I whispered, then I sprang out of the bush as hot air blasted off my back.

"FIRE!" I bellowed, hoping my act was convincing as I attempted to 'gasp for breath.' "Fire! They're evacuating the place!"

With perfect timing, the fire's smoke set off an alarm in the library. People screamed, and steps pounded as they raced out of the library as fast as they could.

The men's eyes widened and gazed behind me to see smoke pouring out of the bushes and flames licking the grass.

"Go, go, go!" I screamed, darting as fast as I could to the other side. "Unless you want to be caught in the middle of this, let a wizard handle this, but until the wizards are here, we need to *leave!*"

The men didn't need to be told twice. They took off running as fast as they could, abandoning the books they were loading and the truck.

I sprinted back to Phoenix once the last of them disappeared; she was grinning. "Okay, that was pretty good," she admitted as I followed her into the library.

My annoyed response got stuck in my throat as we walked in. I inhaled sharply, marveling at the biggest library in the world.

"Whoa," I whispered as my eyes ran over large bookshelf after bookshelf after bookshelf. Everything was made with marble, and the crystal chandelier and grand staircases made me feel like I was in a castle, except instead of furniture, there were bookshelves.

"How are we ever going to find it?" I asked.

Phoenix rolled her eyes. "Librarian, *duh.*"

"Everyone thinks there was a fire. I doubt a librarian would hang around."

"Oh, yeah?" Phoenix looked past me with a smugly raised eyebrow.

I turned around to find a woman that was the perfect image of a librarian. She had white hair that wrapped into a tight bun. Her skin hung because of its wrinkles, and stormy gray eyes bulged on her face. Beaded glasses hung from her neck, and her hands rested over her simple blouse, which was beige.

"Weird," I frowned, but Phoenix pulled me along. We made our way to the woman, who seemed to be staring straight through us. I waved my hand in front of her face. "Hello?"

The woman looked at me and smiled with thin lips. "Hello, son. How can I help you? Are you looking for a specific book?"

"Uh, yeah, actually," I answered, taken aback. "*Powerful Artifacts of Arma*. It's supposed to be very old. Do you know where that would be?"

"Hmm, I don't think so," the librarian smiled. She curled her long fingers, and that's when I got a good look at her tall, green fingernails. Phoenix looked like she was about to throw up.

We waited for a moment, but nothing happened.

"Strange, the book always comes when I do that." Oddly, the librarian didn't seem all that surprised. "There must be something wrong with the spell. I have been trying to collect my missing books, but I never seem to be able to call on that certain book. I suppose you'll just have to look manually."

"Alright, then," Phoenix said, her eyes still fixed on the librarian's revolting fingernails. "Can you just tell us where the historical section *P* is?" It was as good a place to start as any.

\*\*\*

The pile of books towered so high, I couldn't see where I was going. I kept my eyes on the middle book, which was placed so far to the right, it threatened to fall and take the entire stack down with it, leaving books sprawled all over the floor.

"Seamus, hurry up!" Phoenix called from somewhere ahead of me. "We haven't got all day, you know!"

I barely managed to follow her voice, nearly smashing into a bookshelf and running straight into a chair before finally getting to Phoenix. I dropped the books on the table in front of her and sighed with relief, massaging my aching arms.

"Next time, you're carrying the books and I'm yelling about how long you're taking," I told her as she grabbed a book, ignoring me.

"At least we only have to look at the covers," Phoenix reassured me as she left it to the side. I ambled to the nearest shelf. Between *Past, Present, and Future* by Bo Towier and *Poztein's Adventures* by Josephine Foreman, there was nothing.

"Why couldn't there just be a *P-O-W-E-R-F-U-L* section so we could find it straightaway?" I complained.

"Keep looking," Phoenix ordered, incapable of tearing her eyes away from the mountain of books she was going through. "It has to be here somewhere."

"But that's just it," I told her, sitting down. Phoenix glanced up and frowned at me. "Why wouldn't Calypso check here? It would've been so easy just to grab the book and leave. And why couldn't the librarian summon the book when she tried?"

"Maybe Calypso doesn't know about the book, Seamus. And as for the librarian, you have to know the place of the book to summon it." Phoenix rolled her eyes, like this was obvious.

"Then why did she act surprised when it didn't come?"

"I don't know, but how does it matter? We have to find that book, and unless you have any other ideas, we better get back to work."

I sighed as she grabbed another book and put it away. I made my way to the bookshelves and took another book that was labeled *Parallel Locks: Famous Secret Rooms of History* by G.L. Thomson.

"*Famous Secret Rooms of History*, huh?" I muttered to myself, a sly grin spreading across my face. I peeked at Phoenix, who was still deep in search, and then dropped my eyes down to the book.

"Er, Phoenix?" I called.

Phoenix looked up from her book, her eyes bright. "You've found something?" she asked hopefully.

"Well, no. I just wanted to tell you that I need to use the restroom," I said, feeling a little guilty. Explaining that *Famous Secret Rooms of History* could help us wasn't worth the effort. Besides, there was something freeing about following my hunch on my own, and if it worked out, she'd forget about being mad.

Probably.

Hopefully.

"Oh." Phoenix sank back down into her chair glumly. "Okay. I'll keep looking."

I took *Famous Secret Rooms of History* and stood up, leaving our table to go to one all the way on the other side of the library, near the bathrooms. It was a long walk, and it took me fifteen minutes just to get there.

As soon as I reached, I set the book down on the table and started flipping through it, muttering its contents to myself. A few pages in, I realized the entire book was made up of entries.

A couple of them were particularly gripping, one of those being about a prisoner sailing somewhere far away.

*1776, Philippines*

*Waters are getting rougher every day. The Philippines are not too far away, and it's too late to turn back for Lucy and little baby Alice. Want Alice to grow up well-kept with good schooling and good meals to keep her healthy. Still a prisoner on the Dolphin, but still the only one who knows anything about sailing. Have to find the secret room full of riches before escaping. I might die out here, but when the Ranger comes 'round I'll have a much better chance at surviving.*

The weird part about the entry was it was about a place called the Philippines, but I knew for a fact there was no such place in Arma.

*I'm probably just blanking,* I reassured myself, because if these entries weren't true, then neither were their secret rooms. I looked below the entry to find something even more exciting.

*I found the secret room last night in the chambers when Dan and Harry were asleep. I'm working on the plan to help all the prisoners escape, but the riches (millions of dollars) I will keep to myself. For Lucy and Alice, I will do anything.*

*HOW TO UNLOCK THE SECRET ROOM:*

*The door was hidden in the wall. There was a lever hidden in the wall that I finally found. When I pulled it, the doors opened, and I was able to get inside. I finally got the treasure, and all the prisoners can finally escape. I can't wait to see Lucy and Alice back home.*

I looked up at the bathroom. Secret room? If there was a secret room, where would it be?

*This is the biggest library in the world. How am I supposed to find a secret room?* I wondered to myself. Then, it hit me. *Biggest library in the world.* And the biggest library in the world would have the most books, right? Everything on anything.

So, how hard would a book full of magic spells be to find?

I raced through the bookshelves, not bothering to be quiet about it. Where was the *Potions* section?

*Spells, Ancient Runes, Astrology...* There! *Potions!*

I searched like my life depended on it. Finally, I found a section of beginners' potions and snatched as many books as I could off the shelf, not bothering to pick them up, instead letting them fall to the ground.

I crouched down on the floor, searching through the books until I found one that looked promising: *Simmering Cauldron, For Beginners* by Garold Dursay.

I paged through it as fast as I could until I found what I was searching for:

*Location potions only work on objects. Anything with life, such as plants or animals, will not be found using any location potions. If an object has been purposely hidden, a location spell can uncover where it is, but if the object has protecting spells on it, or any kind of magical barrier, this potion will not work, and neither will any other. While you are chanting the words, be careful to concentrate on what you are saying. The potion will be finished when the last ingredient is placed inside the cauldron.*

As soon as I finished reading, a cauldron appeared. I dashed to the bookshelf, where there was a cabinet stuck to it that contained potions' ingredients. A sign that had big letters on it said BEGINNER POTIONS PERMITTED ONLY. I swung open the cabinet and grabbed everything I needed, carrying it back to the table.

I filled the cauldron with lukewarm water from the bathroom and added the ingredients, carefully, following the instructions step by step. Soon, the potion was ready. I took two spoonfuls and poured them carefully into a vial. Then I shook the vial a bit before dropping (and this part had to be precise) two drops on to the words— *Powerful Artifacts of Arma.*

The words glowed yellow, and sparks began to fly from them. I stumbled from the letters, trying to squint through the newfound light. A bright flash of blue blinded me, and I yelped as I shielded my eyes. The blue light gathered itself up until it was a rotating ball of light, floating in midair. All of a sudden, it let off a huge amount of white light and flew right into my chest, all the light disappearing with it.

Uh… was that supposed to happen?

Suddenly, I felt the erratic urge to go to the *Astronomy* section. Thinking tempestuously that this was the potion, I sprinted breathlessly to *Astronomy* and let the tracking potion tell me where to go. I shut my eyes and grasped a blue book with a picture of a planet on it, pulling it out of its place on the bookshelf.

A grinding sound erupted, and the wall that the bookshelf was pushed against split into two. Before I could really understand what was happening, the wall was gone, and all that was there was an opening into a room.

A weird noise that sounded like a mouse squeaking mixed with a dog growling came from my throat. In front of me was a small, lusterless room made of cold cobblestone. Sunlight shone through the window on the right, and green vines twisted around the bookshelves and floor.

I let out a shallow breath as I gingerly strode in. The wall grinded close behind me, and where an opening once was, in replacement was a large, wooden door.

Frowning, I circled around and peered over the books. A thick coat of dust covered almost everything. It felt like no one had been down there in a very long time.

I rushed up the spiraling stairs that creaked under my feet. I prudently took a book out of its place on the bookshelf and placed it on to a wooden desk. I flipped the book open and started reading.

"*Powerful Artifacts of Arma,*" I whispered, placing the book back where it belonged, next to the other books.

All of a sudden, a strange thumping sound came from the back of the room, as if something was trying to escape from its place on the bookshelf. An ancient-looking book with a crumbling cover and yellowed pages zipped out from behind the bookshelves. It flew across the room, whizzing through the bookshelves, and stopped right in front of me, floating in midair.

I widened my eyes, amazed at the sight before me. The fading letters on the cover of the book read: *Powerful Artifacts of Arma*.

No. Way.

Did I just summon *Powerful Artifacts of Arma*?

There was absolutely no way.

Gingerly, I took the old book in my hands, and I almost fell forward when the full weight of the book buried itself into my palms.

"Argh!" I grunted as I shifted my weight accordingly. I barely made it down the stairs and to the desk with the book. Heaving it on to the crooked wood, the first thing I did was flip to the last page and widen my eyes at the number of pages: *four thousand nine hundred and ninety-six!* How long would it take to write such a big book?

But then another thought hit me: How was I going to find the page about the Roses of Arma?

The answer came to me immediately. I grabbed my potions book and flipped it to the page about the location potion. I gathered my ingredients once more (I found everything I needed in a small cabinet behind the bookshelf) and mixed the potion again. Then I dropped a few drops from a vial on to the words I wrote – "Roses of Arma" - and they glowed brightly. Sparks flew from it once more, and to my great surprise, the page set itself on fire and burnt itself to crisps. Its ashes glowed red. I yelped and screamed, "What the—!"

I frowned, touching the page with my fingertip. Did I do something wrong? Why had it caught fire this time?

All of a sudden, *Powerful Artifacts of Arma* flipped open, like an invisible hand had touched it. One single page in the book glowed yellow. I read what the page said.

*Roses of Arma and their origins*

I stared at the page, my eyes wide. Everything was there. It went on for twelve pages.

I had found what we were looking for!

*Before* Calypso.

I carefully ripped the twelve pages and folded them into my pocket. I felt guilty for desecrating a historic epitome, but one, I did not have time to copy twelve pages, and two, I did not want to leave it behind for Calypso to find, in case she ever figured out the path to the secret room. Then I turned towards the door and tried the handle. It swung open easily.

Quietly, I closed the door, one hand in my pocket to make sure the pages wouldn't magically disappear. Then I raced past the magic section and back to the history section, where Phoenix was still deep in search.

"Phoenix!" I yelled, waving my arms wildly. "Guess what I found?"

Phoenix took one look at my wide smile and grinned. "Really? You've got it?" She looked at my hands, frowning. "It must be a really small book if it fits in your pocket."

"Oh, no, it's the opposite. It was nearly five thousand pages…" I smiled at her wide eyes, feeling joy from her excitement, "therefore I couldn't bring it."

"Seriously?" She rolled her eyes. "Oh, Seamus. What section was it under?"

"It wasn't under a section," I explained as she got up.

"Then where was it?"

I tried to explain about the astronomy book that was really a lever, and the secret door that opened when I pulled it, but I could tell I wasn't doing a very good job of explaining it when Phoenix scrunched up her eyebrows, cocked her head, and asked, "Wait, so the wall gave away and the book was waiting there, floating for you?"

My face reddened. "Not exactly. I think it's better if I show you."

I took her to the Astronomy section and searched the shelves for the book with a planet on it. Finally, I found it *waaaaaaay* in the back like I left it, and I grabbed it and pulled. The wall made a grinding noise, and it tore apart, revealing the same room that I had discovered before.

A large book with yellowed pages and dust on its cover rested on the desk pushed against the bookshelf.

"Is that—?" Phoenix gazed at me with her eyes wide.

I nodded.

Slowly, Phoenix approached the desk and brushed her fingers against the cover. "I can't believe it," she whispered. Then she glanced at me. "Alright, now carry this five-thousand-pager."

"What? The *entire* thing?"

"We're not leaving this behind! It's *ancient* and *historic* and obviously tremendously important if someone went to all this trouble—"

"That probably had something to do with the fact that it holds the location of the *Roses*!"

Phoenix scowled at me. "We're taking it."

Glaring at her, I wrapped my arms around it and managed to lift it off the desk. I wheezed, gasping for breath. The book was no easy feat, but I managed to carry it (with no help from Phoenix, of course) back to the librarian's desk. When I finally dropped the book on the table, I massaged my arms woefully.

"We better hurry," Phoenix said, poking me with her finger and pointing up. "People will start coming back inside any minute now."

"May I help you?" The old librarian came hobbling back behind her desk. "Oh, hello, you two. Did you..." The librarian's voice dropped a bit. "find that book you were looking for?"

I frowned at Phoenix, and she shrugged. "Actually, yes," I told her, showing her *Powerful Artifacts of Arma*. "Can we check this out? I haven't got a card, but—"

"That book isn't in the system," the librarian interrupted.

"So… ?" I asked.

"So, you may not check out this book," the librarian finished, with a blank expression on her face.

Phoenix gave me a confused look, which I could relate to. What was going on?

"But we talked to you… you *said…*" I stammered, flabbergasted.

Then the librarian turned to me, and I heard Phoenix gasp loudly. My eyes widened and my legs froze, because what looked back at me was not a regular face, but a monster with flaring red eyes, claws the size of rulers, and long legs that were green and furry. Damn. A Calypso implant!

"Oh, really?" I yelled, my knuckles white. "A librarian monster? We've faced packs of wolves with poisonous bites and red eyes! Ha! Do you think a *librarian monster* could scare us?"

The librarian slashed at me with her claws and hissed a nasty growl. I stepped back and screamed, "I WAS WRONG! VERY WRONG! RUUUUNNNNN!"

Easier said than done. Phoenix seized the book and nearly fell over with its weight. The librarian lunged at her, claws out, and she rolled out of the way, barely dodging the monster.

"Leave the book and let's get out of here!"

Phoenix glared at me. *"Are you crazy?"* Why didn't I tell Phoenix I'd torn out the pages? Now I couldn't say it because the librarian was within earshot.

The librarian cackled evilly, creeping closer. "Yes, take the book... It will make my lunch a lot easier to catch..."

I dove out of the way when the librarian lunged at me. Feeling I had no other choice and not enough time to argue, I yelled, "Fine! Take the book and get to Sorin! I'll meet you in the carriage!"

The librarian grabbed at Phoenix, who was attempting to wave her away with her dagger, stepping back.

"What? And leave you here? No way!" Phoenix screamed.

"Phoenix, you stuck with me at the wolves, but I need you to trust me now. Save yourself! *Please!*" I yelled, doing a somersault while narrowly dodging a swipe from the librarian's claws.

"ENOUGH TALKING! YOU WILL HAND OVER THAT ROSE!" The librarian screamed in a shrill voice so terrible, I covered my ears.

Phoenix crawled out from behind the desk without the book and watched me with a hint of a smile playing on her face. "Seamus, if I didn't trust you, you wouldn't be wearing that bag. Now shut up and let me save you like I always do."

Before I could protest, the librarian lunged at both of us, and we whirled out of the way in opposite directions. I grasped Alexander's sword and willed it to turn into a dagger. Phoenix unsheathed her gleaming dagger as well.

The librarian turned towards me. I gulped down the fear in my throat, reminding myself over and over again that I was chosen for this. Then, summoning all the strength and courage I had in me, I shouted, "Hey, dirt face! Come and get me!"

Someone should have mentioned, it's never fun playing hide and seek with a crazy librarian who wants you dead.

I raced through the shelves, zigzagging through the tables and chairs, with the librarian on my tail. For an old woman, she was surprisingly fast.

I stole a quick look behind me. The librarian was now even angrier, kicking tables over like they were nothing and rattling bookshelves as she passed. In the corner of my vision, I could barely make out Phoenix, stomping her way up a grand staircase.

*Save me, huh? You mean save yourself?* But all those feelings were forgotten when a sharp knife whizzed past me, nearly cutting my ear off. I turned around, shocked, and ducked before another knife took my head off.

I ran for my life.

I veered to the right, almost banging straight into a bookshelf. But then, the most shocking thing ever happened.

A storm of fireballs rained down to the right of me, burning the books to crisps of nothing but black ashes of paper. I yelped and instinctively dove behind a shelf, breathing hard as I tried to get a good view of what was happening.

The librarian's face conflicted with confusion and ire, frowning at the ceiling, as if wondering when the weatherman changed the forecast.

I squinted up the staircase, following the steps to the large, balcony-like platform that hovered twenty feet above the ground. On it was a figure I could barely make out, but there was no doubt it was Phoenix. Her hands blazed with flames as she directed shots of fire straight at the librarian, setting the tables, chairs, and all the books into a lively blaze.

"ARGH!" The librarian screamed as she lunged for me from behind the bookshelves, dodging the fireballs. Caught by surprise, I yowled as she pounced on me, her claws digging into my skin. The insufferable pain of it blared in my head, and my focus blurred as I struggled to stay conscious.

Then, in one gracious second, the pain lifted, the force of it pushing me over on to my side. I groaned as my focus sharpened, and I froze in horror when I saw the librarian screaming with agony, her right arm absorbed in bright, orange flames.

I gasped for air, turning my head away from the librarian and looking back at Phoenix, who was rushing down the steps towards me. I could barely keep my eyes open as my head fell to the ground, catching sight of three big gashes that made me feel sick. Squeezing my eyes shut, I managed to turn my head away from my arm and look up at Phoenix, who was now on the ground, rushing towards me.

"Seamus!" Phoenix gasped and covered her mouth. She summed up courage and whispered, "Can you stand?"

"I think so," I answered weakly, knowing by the mortified look on Phoenix's face that I must look bad. "How do I look?" I asked, nevertheless.

Phoenix shook her head as she got under my arm, and leaning on her, I managed to get to my feet.

Well, at least she was being honest.

People had started streaming back into the library, smiling, laughing, and snapping pictures, even though there was a very clear sign outside that read: NO PICTURES.

"Come on," she said as crazy alarms went off again in the distance. "We need to get to the carriage so I can figure out a way to mix up a brew that will heal you."

A wave of nausea made me stumble to the bookshelf, hitting my head on the hardwood. Swallowing, I nodded, and managed to get back on my feet.

"Are you sure you can walk?"

Annoyance swept over me. "I can take care of myself," I muttered a little more harshly than I meant to. Phoenix was unperturbed. She was used to putting up with my stubbornness.

We made our way to the doors of the St. Henderson library so slowly, a snail could have sped past us. As we made our way through the ashes of paper and remaining crisps of chairs, I glared at the books bitterly. Phoenix left me for a moment to retrieve our four thousand ninety-six page tome where she had hidden it. When she got back, she continued dragging me with one hand and the book, about equally heavy, with the other.

It felt like hours, but finally, we got outside to the parking lot. Since my arms felt like they were falling off, Phoenix helped me into the carriage, and, ignoring Sorin's happy whinnies, climbed in after me.

"Don't worry, I'll figure this out," Phoenix swore, but the lines etched on her forehead told me otherwise. Her fingers trembled as she reached into her pocket and took out her small notebook. She flipped through it and rummaged around the back of the carriage, searching for supplies.

My eyes slowly closed, and the torturous pain of the cuts overwhelmed me. I groaned and barely heard myself croak, "Phoenix…" before everything went black.

# FOURTEEN

**"Seamus,"** a soft voice whispered.

My eyes opened laboriously. The first thing I noticed was a bitter taste in my mouth, like I had swallowed a rotten egg.

My throat erupted with hacking coughs as I gagged. "What…" I sucked in a huge breath, "what *is* that?"

*"Seamus!"* Phoenix threw her arms around me and grasped me in the tightest hug ever. My eyes probably bulged as I choked on the air that I sucked in.

"Phoenix," I strained. "Are you trying to kill me?"

That made Phoenix drop me on the lumpy seat and lour at me with her hands on her hips. "I'm going to ignore you criticizing my hugs just because you passed out."

"What did you *give* me?" I gasped, sticking out my tongue from my mouth. "It's like I just ate a bunch of rotten eggs."

Phoenix scowled at me. "It was a very *difficult* and extremely *complicated* healing potion. No need to thank me for saving your life, though, of course."

I grinned, elbowing her at her haughty expression. She glanced back at me, surprised, then turned away again, although it was obvious, she was expecting something.

"Thank you, Phoenix," I told her solemnly. "I guess I owe you one."

Phoenix turned around, new joy in her eyes. "*Two*, by my count. I got the librarian off you as well."

"Yeah, but I saved you from the shadows and the wolves. You saved me from the roc and the librarian, so that means I just owe you one," I bargained.

"Have you really been keeping track of all our life-or-death moments?"

"Have you not?"

"Good point," Phoenix agreed, standing up from her seat. "Well, it seems you're alright. It should be a fast recovery from here on out. By the time we get to Circe and Zia, you'll be good as new and ready to kick some more monster booty."

"Wait, what? Circe and Zia?"

"The pages that you tore from probably the most important book in Arma said so. I don't know why they put the Rose in Circe, but Zia's at the end of Arma. I'd never even heard of it before. That sounds like a good place to hide a Rose," Phoenix explained keenly.

I wasn't sure I could share her zest. We'd only secured one Rose so far, out of *three*. Even though there was only one Rose inside my backpack, Phoenix reminded us that we had been through *four* life-threatening situations. How were we expected to survive two more Roses?

"Phoenix…" I started, but when I looked up, Phoenix was gone, and the carriage had already started moving.

My fingers clasped the seat as I wondered if I'd made a hideous mistake. I had almost lost Phoenix way too many times, and we'd been in too many close situations.

I wanted to give up.

Then and there.

*So* bad.

I wanted to stalk up to Glavio, hand him the Rose, and say, "Well, we tried. Why don't you take your turn saving the world?"

But I *couldn't*. The truth was, nobody wanted to be the hero. Nobody could understand the tremendous strain and difficulty it came with unless they were there, earning the rite of passage. I'd been at it for only a few days, and every part of me wanted to throw my hands up and surrender.

But lives were at stake, the fate of Arma… . How could I bear letting them down? If there was some slim chance of success, how could I just toss it away? Even if the prophecy never mentioned me, would it have been possible for me to stand aside, doing nothing?

Some *lucky* people could do that.

But unfortunately, I wasn't one of them.

***

The greenery of Circe approached alarmingly fast. The carriage shook so hard that a cushion escaped from the back and fell right on my head. I clutched the handle of the carriage the best I could without opening the door.

"PHOENIX!" I howled as another cushion catapulted towards me, forcing me to duck underneath the seat. "WHAT THE HECK ARE YOU DOING?"

Phoenix's face looked back at me, a concerned, nervous face peeking through the window. But another swerve from the carriage made her head whirl back around, and my hip crashed into the wall.

Grunting as the carriage started shaking again, I used my arms to pull myself up, keeping a tight hold on the top of the seat. A large bang resonated through the carriage like an explosion, making me fly backwards and hit my head on the side of the carriage.

Then, unexpectedly, everything went still.

I caught sight of Phoenix, jumping out from the driver's seat and yanking the door open.

"Sorry," Phoenix apologized sheepishly, her hair tussled messily as a result of the ride. She gave me a sly grin. "We ran into a flock of birds."

To my surprise, I grinned.

Despite herself, Phoenix grinned too. "Nice to see the old Seamus back," she teased as I climbed down from the carriage with my backpack that held the first delicate Rose.

"So, the Rose is in the woods?" I asked, frowning uncertainly at the long stretch of bushy-topped trees. "It's even bigger than the Olin Woods. How are we even supposed to find anything in there, assuming we manage to search the entire thing?"

"Good question," Phoenix said. "More so with Calypso chasing us."

"Of course," I agreed. "So, what are we waiting for?"

"How about a break?"

"Stop complaining," I strode past her with an exaggerated roll of my eyes, "and start searching for the trail. For all we know, Calypso might be on our heels for this Rose."

"You know what I think?" Phoenix hurried, quickening her step to catch up with mine. "I think Calypso cares about the Roses, but she cares as much about you. She desperately needs you to join her army. We don't know why, but that is evident."

I glared at her, perplexed. "I wouldn't call it caring!" I said angrily, trying to steady the emotion in my straining voice. "She was fine killing me if I didn't cooperate with her!"

She was fine with killing Phoenix, too.

A pang inside me told me that the pain Calypso had left behind that day would never leave me. It stayed buried inside me, under mounds and mounds of fear, anger, and grief.

"She obviously wanted you on her side desperately. Desperate enough to kidnap us, and then agree to let me live in exchange for your cooperation. When you agreed, you revealed your weakness. She wants to capture you and use me to get you to work for her. There's no doubt she'll try to capture us after we collect all three Roses for the double reward—the Roses and you. If she succeeds, she'll seal the fate of wizarding magic *and* whatever importance you are to this entire thing."

No words.

I wanted to tell her she was crazy. I wanted to make fun of her for her convoluted thinking. I wanted to tell her that was stupid, if not crazy, and she shouldn't be so fatalistic, because it kind of freaked me out.

But I couldn't. Because the problem was…

She was right.

I didn't tell her that, though. We walked in silence, my stomach squirming as I turned Phoenix's words around in my head. like I used to turn chocolate inside my mouth. No part of the delicious sweet would go untouched. Except, this was more like a bitter, rotting piece of celery.

Calypso knew something I didn't. Glavio too.

*Seamus, you don't know it yet, but you're meant for so much more than you think. You're destined to be a hero, and even if it is always a risky path in life, it's clear that's what you're meant to be.*

That's what Glavio told me. Too many secrets.

I thought it was all an exaggeration. I thought that if we succeeded in getting the Roses, we'd go our merry way. Probably return to our parents, back to our normal life.

Now I realized *I* was being ridiculous. There was no way, with all the facts set in front of me, that it was all going to end after this.

I guess I had known that all along, but I never really wanted to admit it.

I wasn't going home.

I wasn't living a normal life.

Maybe not ever.

All of a sudden, the clarity was dizzying. It felt like someone had dunked my head in ice-cold water.

"Don't worry," Phoenix promised, her expression telling me she wished she had never said anything as she rested her hand on my shoulder. "I'll help you on whatever quest you go on."

"So, this probably won't be super easy. But look on the bright side. We know that the Rose probably looks like the one we found before. Crystal petals, golden stem," she said, bringing me back to the present.

I glanced at her. "How are you so calm about this?"

Then, in one quick glimpse, the mask covering her face faltered, allowing fear and doubt to flicker across her expression. But as soon as it appeared, it vanished, letting confidence push through her face once again.

Phoenix rolled her eyes. "I get this sucks," she said, striding next to me and placing a comforting hand on my shoulder, "but, no offence and all, you can be a bit *dramatic.*"

Maybe it *wasn't* a comforting hand. It was a *pitying* hand.

Did my best friend just call me *dramatic?*

Before we could have any more of that conversation, a streak of red whizzed past her, slamming into a tree square in the middle of the trunk. Time slowed down, and in a tense breath, the tree swayed to the right and to the left, before plummeting down straight in between me and Phoenix.

I gazed up at Phoenix with wide eyes. For a moment, neither of us said or did anything, and neither did whatever fired that death-encased spell.

Then I jolted back to my senses. "HIT THE GROUND!" I screamed, and both of us rolled on to the moist dirt as spells above us lit up the sky, streaking past us and kicking trees over.

"SEAMUS!" Phoenix yelled. "LOOK! NEXT TO THE YELLOW BUSH!"

I narrowly dodged a third falling tree.

"THE GLOWING ROSE!"

I squinted through the raining leaves and flying spells to find the gleaming Rose. It had sparkling, crystal petals, and a delicate, golden stem just like the fragile one in the carriage.

Then, out of nowhere, a woman with tangled black hair, warts on her chin, and a long, crumbling dress that was dirty and rumpled rose out of a bush. Her arm stretched out, her hands sporting yellow fingernails that held a despicably long wand that was chipped away at the edges.

Phoenix, responding with action almost immediately, began catapulting as many fireballs as she could muster at the disgusting monstrosity of a witch, with one hand on her dagger. The witch dove out of the way.

"Just get to the Rose!" I roared, shooting a sharp icicle at the bushes where the witch had disappeared into.

The witch popped back up and grinned evilly at us. Before either of us could react, she whirled to the tree next to her and shot a streak of black at the tree.

"Behold," she thundered, "and bask in my greatness as you die a very painful death... by my friend!"

As she said that, the ground began to shake and rumble, and a boatload of leaves rained from the sky. I gasped, losing my balance and being swept off my feet and on to the ground, groaning as the whole of Arma trembled under my feet.

I managed to squint through the falling branches and hurricane of leaves to catch a glance of what was causing the tremor, but when I found out, I felt like kicking a tree.

There, in the midst of all of the chaos, was a tree monster.

# FIFTEEN

"Oh, no," Phoenix muttered."

I clutched the handle of Alexander's sword and unsheathed the centuries-old blade. Phoenix tightened her grip on her gleaming dagger.

"Okay." I took a deep breath. "Let's fight this tree—"

I was interrupted when a spell came straight at me. I dove to the ground and tumbled into a roll to dodge it.

"We're supposed to fight the witch *and* the tree monster?"

The tree monster roared, shaking the ground around it, and uprooted a tree as easily as if it were a small tin can, chucking the fifty-foot tree straight at us.

"RUN!" Phoenix bellowed.

We bolted as fast as we could, zigzagging and jumping to avoid the spells and the falling trees.

"Light a fire!" I yelled.

"No! It might destroy the Rose if I lose control! And we're in the middle of the *woods*!"

She was right. There was no way Phoenix's fire would help us in this situation. Not just that, but our weapons were pretty useless. It was a fifty-foot tall *tree*. What were we going to do, slice some bark off?

"Okay!" I panted, trying to catch my breath and steady my racing heart as the sound of a large tree stomping sent my ears ringing. "I'm going to need you to distract the tree monster while I try to ice it to the ground so it can't move."

"No! Bad plan! What am I supposed to do? I can't use my powers or my weapon!"

"You have to figure something out! Use your dagger. Spark up a little bit of flames that are easy to control. Do something. Anything! Just buy me some time."

She breathed hard. "Okay, go!"

I bolted out into the battlefield, where falling trees became a regular occurrence. Swerving, dodging, and leaping over trees, I managed to reach the base of the tree monster. The tree monster bellowed a mighty roar and swiped its branch-arms down at me, causing me to slide beneath its long branches to avoid it.

"PHOENIX!" I screamed. "NOW!"

But before Phoenix could race out of her hiding spot and distract the tree monster, the tree monster, who was very annoyed at this point, dove its branches down at me, swiping me up in its bark-covered claws.

"ARGH!" I grunted as I was raised into the air. "HELP!"

Phoenix raced out of her hiding spot with her dagger unleashed, ready for battle. She swiped at the tree's trunk, although it didn't do much damage, since it was a *tree*.

Meanwhile, I was stuck in the painfully rough claws of a tree, wondering what I possibly could do to escape the powerful grip of a branch. Squinting down at Phoenix's feeble attempts to defeat the tree, I hollered angrily, "JUST GET ITS ATTENTION! IT'S A TREE! MAYBE IT'S AFRAID OF SQUIRRELS!"

"THAT'S THE STUPIDEST THING I'VE EVER HEARD!"

"HAVE YOU GOT ANY BETTER IDEAS?"

"USE YOUR POWER!"

*I can do this, I can do this, I can do this.*

With a deep breath, I gathered my concentration, and trying to block out the rest of the world, I summoned all the water and cold inside of me I could manage. It's extremely difficult to ice something quickly when the rest of the world is falling apart. By the looks of how many trees fell down per second, I doubted the Rose Woods would exist by the end of this.

I touched the bark of the tree and felt it grow colder and colder, until the cold turned the water particles into ice. The tree, being a tree, didn't feel anything at the start, but as the ice began to spread to the rest of its branches and body, it began to shake its leaves in a frenzied fit.

The situation would have been almost funny if it had not been for the fact that the monster wanted to kill us all and I was in the grasps of its woody arms.

As my spirits soared higher, the ice spread faster and formed stronger. Everyone's power comes from someplace. Mine comes from my spirit.

Soon, the tree monster was encased in ice. Phoenix, dodging a well-aimed spell from the witch who I had almost forgotten about, watched with big eyes as the tree swayed to the left and right before finally being rooted to the ground and rendered a normal tree again.

Personally, I preferred it that way.

*Looks like one of my dumb ideas worked,* I thought angrily to myself.

"SEAMUS!" Phoenix screamed. "WATCH OUT!"

But it was too late. A purple streak of magic was fired at the branch I clung to. The tree swayed, and a loud, cracking sound filled my ears as I held tightly for dear life. Before I could process what was happening, or understand the death-deep pit in my heart telling me to scream, I felt my body go limp as I plummeted to the ground.

I screamed as I fell, and terror ripped through me as I tumbled down from one branch to another. With nothing between me and the hard ground, and a certain death on contact, my instincts took over.

Fortunately, I had summoned enough water that when I shot a column of water to the ground, enough volume appeared instantly to let me sink in, arresting the velocity of my fall and allowing me to gently float to the ground. As soon as I reached the ground, I directed all that water towards the bushes where the purple streak of magic came from.

"Auooohia," she blabbered in panic, as she was flushed out, with hands and legs flailing, trying to find some footing. It was satisfying to see the smugness wiped off her face with the terror of drowning taking over for an instant.

"We have to win this battle now, before she realizes that the water will just give her a good bath and drain away in a few seconds," I said, without a clue as to how to do that. The witch was too powerful and her wand too potent for us to win a head-on fight.

Phoenix arrived at the same conclusion of the need to win now, but with an actual plan to achieve that goal. A perfectly-timed dagger shot pinned the witch's wand to a nearby tree, neutralizing her weapon. Without the wand, her power was greatly diminished. Flustered and isolated, she was left with no option but to flee. With hatred and vengeance in her eyes, screaming threats of future consequences, she vanished into thin air. We finally breathed, happy to be alive for the moment.

"Was Calypso behind all of this?" Phoenix asked the question I was thinking.

I picked myself up and dusted myself off like nothing had happened. I strode over to the stump, where, miraculously, the Rose floated, unharmed.

Carefully, I took it from its place. For a moment, I gazed at it with awe. There was no doubt it was breathtaking.

"Let's go," I finally said, cradling the Rose in my arms. "Now. We only need one more Rose before we're done with this quest."

# SIXTEEN

**As the carriage rumbled**, I watched the backpack that held two of the most important magical artifacts in the world.

Yet I felt so empty. Like there was a hollow cave inside of me. Like there was no point in this quest at all.

I didn't know why I felt like that. I should've felt triumphant. I should've felt victorious.

Okay, fine.

I *did* know why.

I just didn't want to admit it to myself.

The ride to Zia would be the shortest one we'd traveled so far. Circe and Zia are both near the boundaries of each kingdom, basically almost right next to each other, so it was the most efficient aerial path to bounce from queendom to queendom.

At first, I started out driving, and after an hour, we switched. Neither of us ate much or spoke much. We were running alarmingly low on food. In a couple of days, if we didn't reach Zia fast, we might be eating pincushions. Sorin had been fed the most out of the three of us. Not just because he was the one getting us to Zia, but because neither of us felt right depriving him of food when he hadn't asked to go on this journey.

However, Sorin understood that we were doing something dangerous. Hard to forget the day he saved both of our lives when we were being attacked by a pack of wolves. Phoenix had seriously bonded with Sorin.

All of a sudden, the carriage arched into a dive, and my stomach turned upside down. I remembered the last time, when Phoenix ran into a flock of birds, and wondered if it was a similar situation.

But surprisingly, this time the carriage landed smoothly on the soft grass of Zia.

Finally.

It was *so* close.

The last Rose.

The end of our quest.

But, between us and the last Rose was a barricade of guards, marching up and down. Three of the guards stopped and glowered at us like just landing there was a crime. For all I knew, maybe it was.

Sorin whinnied nervously as I climbed out of the carriage, the backpack still safely stashed away in a well-concealed hiding spot under my seat. Of course, that wouldn't help much if Calypso or her cronies came around. Just like Phoenix, they could probably sense the power trail the Roses let off.

"Excuse me?" Phoenix glared at each of the guards defiantly. "Can you let us through? We're trying to meet our parents in Zia, and they'll get worried if we don't show."

"*You* two are siblings?" the guard questioned.

He had a point. I have black hair, blue eyes, and pearly white skin. Phoenix has light brown hair, amber eyes, and darker skin, like she was born on a beach. We looked nothing like each other.

"He's adopted," Phoenix added quickly.

The guard didn't seem to buy it. "Sorry, miss, but you are *waaaaay* too young to drive a carriage like that. I'm going to have to confiscate it."

Confiscate? *What?*

My mind panicked. *Breathe,* I thought over and over again. *Breathe!*

There was a tense silence, me measuring how hard it would be to take out all ten guards, Phoenix probably analyzing different, smarter, ideas to get past them, while the guards prepared themselves for a confrontation.

As well trained as we were, Phoenix and I weren't superheroes. We wouldn't be able to take on ten armed, well-trained guards, who clearly were not underestimating what we could possibly do.

Phoenix nodded slightly at me. I knew what she was signaling.

I braced myself.

"Look," Phoenix tried once more, "this carriage isn't ours. Please, can you return it to Hes—SEAMUS NOW!"

I unsheathed Alexander's sword and stabbed the ground, a powerful spring of hot water bursting out of the ground.

*Why did I do that?* I wondered to myself as a faint feeling trickled through me. Water springs, especially ones that powerful, were not exactly an easy move. Still, I managed to hold it together as Phoenix erupted in flames. All of this commotion was enough to distract the guards.

"GET IN!" Phoenix screamed.

The guards realized what was going to happen far too late.

I bolted for the driver's seat, and Phoenix tumbled into the back of the carriage. The guards raced after us, but I clasped the reins in my fingers, and Sorin, who had been casually grazing, was not ready for action.

I flicked the reins as fast as I could, the guards so close they could jump into the carriage if they wanted to.

"SORIN, FLY!" I yelled.

He took off into the sky as fast as a bullet, leaving the guards scampering and yelling inaudibly at us from the ground.

I let go of the reins, breathing hard.

"Sorin," I panted, "well done."

Sorin neighed, and I had a feeling that the proud horse had just tried to tell me that he knew that.

"Phoenix!" I called, knocking on the back carriage window that was behind me. "Can you sense the trail of power coming from the Rose? We're going to have to track it from the sky. Landing is trouble, and it won't be long before guards start tracking us even in air."

"I can't from up here!" Phoenix yelled back.

"Why not?"

"The wind, the sky, the clouds—I won't be able to concentrate!"

"Well, you'll have to! We do not have much time. The guards will be on us any minute."

I squinted and scanned the ground with difficulty. I could see guards already scurrying across the landscape.

Phoenix bit her lips nervously. She slowly closed her eyes, attempting to concentrate with the wind booming in her ears. We waited there for five minutes, me losing hope, fearing we were never going to be able to track the Rose.

Then Phoenix's face lit up. "I've got something! Let me take the reins!"

Obediently, I agreed and managed to climb through the window behind me. "Hurry!" I rushed Phoenix, who climbed into the driver's seat.

Suddenly, the carriage jolted forward, and I could hear Phoenix yelling, "Hyah!" in the front.

A small smile managed to squirm its way on to my face.

*We're almost done*, I thought hopefully as I watched the beauty of the landscape speeding by. *One more Rose, and we'd have survived our quest* and *saved the magic of the world. Win-win.*

*Sort of.*

I softly placed my hand on the backpack that carried the weight of two very important Roses. Two very important Roses *we* had managed to save.

Then, a huge jerk of the carriage hitting the ground shook and bumped me within, and the carriage conspicuously slanted as my stomach lurched forward.

Finally, the carriage slowed to a stop, and eagerly, I kicked open the door and sprang out of the carriage with the backpack slung over my shoulder.

Phoenix was already buckling up her boots. She reached for Sorin, who was skittish. "Look, Sorin, we may take a while. You see those woods over there?" Phoenix pointed to the large woods that were impossible to miss. "The Rose is somewhere in there. If we aren't back by nightfall, go looking for us, okay?" She unlatched him from the carriage and fed him a carrot affectionately.

"Come on, Phoenix," I hissed impatiently. "Where's the Rose?"

Phoenix gazed at the vast woods for a good minute. "Somewhere in those woods."

"Are you kidding?"

Phoenix glared at me, making me wish I hadn't said anything. "No, Seamus, I'm *not* kidding. The Rose is somewhere in those woods. I'm going to try to pinpoint the closer area it's in, but right now that's all I have."

She closed her eyes in concentration. I watched her intently, waiting for any better answer than '*the woods.*'

She opened her eyes brightly. "I've a trail! Follow me!"

She raced into the woods, and taking one last glance at Sorin, who grazed in the soft grass, I trekked after her.

We raced past tall trees and large vines tangled in bushes galore. The psychological effects of the tree monster hadn't completely worn off. I eyed each of them, hoping their roots wouldn't become legs and branches become arms.

Then, all of a sudden, Phoenix skirted to a stop. I almost ran straight into her, but I managed to stumble into a clumsy stance.

"Is this it?" I asked, breathing hard, bent over with my hands on my knees.

"Seamus," Phoenix whispered softly. "Look."

I frowned, looking up. That's when I saw it. Glowing at the edge of a cliff that hung off on to the sparkling ocean was the last Pillar of Arma, a gracious Rose with crystal petals and golden leaves.

"Wow," I managed. "It's so close. What are we waiting for?"

But Phoenix held her arm out, blocking me, and shook her head. "It's too easy."

"That's right," a voice I strangely recognized cackled. "It's far too easy, Phoenix. Maybe you were worth sparing."

That's when I placed the voice.

Panic and terror ripped through me as I stumbled back, whirling my head to search for the source.

*No.*

Not again!

A gasp broke the stretched seconds of silence.

A woman, concealed in the brush of the woods, revealed herself. She looked exactly like she had in the dimly lit room where she had chained me to a chair and threatened Phoenix's life.

Bad memories flooded through my mind.

A vivid vision of the cold, shuddering room and the chains that tied me to the chair crashed through my mind as Calypso's mortifying image strutted in.

*I didn't find much use for her, except maybe dinner for my babies.*

Forcing my eyes open, I caught sight of an entire army of canines trailing behind her. Jackals, wolves, shepherds—every single one more ominous than the last.

"Looks like I finally caught you," she hissed, her lips twisting into a malicious smile.

Frozen.

Every single limb in my body was frozen as if ice had spread across me.

I *should* be immune.

I *should* be the hero.

But I wasn't.

The only plan that drifted through my head was: Stall.

I needed to stall her, but every single conversation that zipped through my head got stuck in my throat as soon as I tried to put it into words.

Swallowing, I sucked in a breath and whispered the question I'd been wondering for ages: "How did you even find the Roses?"

"A little bird told me about the start of your mission." Calypso smiled evilly as I tried desperately to slow my racing breath. "WAD isn't nearly as secure as you think! I tracked you from the moment you left that wizard's protection"

"She was afraid enough of Glavio to leave us alone while we were with him," I thought.

Some part of me wanted to wait for Phoenix to deal with her, but...

I couldn't put her through that.

Phoenix had endured a much worse experience than I had. That was definitely the reason that she stood petrified, her fist still curled loosely around her dagger.

"You managed to escape my shadow monsters. But that was okay. I was toying with you by sending a few shadows at you. It was fun to give you a little scare. I picked up your trail again on your way to Trenton."

"You baited us to find the Rose and planned to swoop in to get both the Rose and me?" I confirmed.

"That was the plan," Calypso admitted, stroking a German shepherd standing next to her. "But to begin with, I'd been searching Trenton for a while. Finding assistance in an expert tracker delayed me. Following you turned out to be easier."

I wanted to clobber her, but I wanted to turn around and bolt at the same time.

*Stall,* I reminded myself. *Stall*

"However, luckily for you, you managed to slip through by fingers again."

Luckily? We beat her fair and square in Trenton.

"I have to admit, you were quire resourceful at the library. Finding and escaping with the *Powerful Artifacts of Arma* was impressive," Calypso cackled. It was clear she was enjoying the moment. But I had no choice but to keep her talking until I came up with a better plan.

"I lost track of you after the library, but the mayhem you created in the Rose Woods was like sending up flares telling the world where you were."

As if we had a choice to do it more subtly with the tree monster and the witch trying to annihilate us.

Everything made sense now.

*We had led her right to us and to all the Roses—two in my bag and one perched up in front of us for Calypso to pluck.*

"Now you decided to show up to finish us and capture the Roses." I mumbled the obvious.

"Precisely," she smiled charmingly. "Get them," she ordered as she flicked her hand, leaning towards her canines. Obediently, they bounded towards us. Alarms went off in my head as Phoenix, who panicked, clutched her dagger with a white hand and I unsheathed my sword.

But before I could swipe the blade at all, a wolf leapt at Phoenix and sunk its teeth into her leg. Phoenix cried out in pain, collapsing to the ground with a thud.

"Phoenix!" I screamed, moving towards her, but a crowd of jackals growled at me, forcing me to stagger back.

Then the dogs dragged Phoenix, who struggled unsuccessfully to lose their strong grip, all the way to Calypso.

Calypso grabbed Phoenix's arm and jolted her up; Phoenix's leg was still limp, and the wounds were visible. Calypso unsheathed a gleaming blade and held its sharp, deadly edge at her throat.

# SEVENTEEN

**Phoenix's eyes were wide with fear,** watching me like she knew this would be her final moment.

Searing panic stacked inside me.

"Seamus…" Phoenix croaked weakly. "Don't…"

I already knew what Calypso was going to ask for.

"The Roses, hero," Calypso demanded. "Or your *friend* is going to kick the bucket a little earlier than she was supposed to."

Phoenix's hands ignited with sparks as she barely breathed, her eyes full of fear, but Calypso pressed the blade harder against her throat.

"*Don't you dare,*" Calypso breathed in her ear.

Phoenix stopped and the flames dispersed.

"Calypso," I begged, my cheeks wet and cold. "Please, don't hurt her. Please let her go. I'll work for you. Anything. *Please.*"

"The *Roses!*" Calypso ordered sharply.

Every scenario, every single detail of every single plan I could come up with, played in my head. If I used the water to try and get rid of Calypso, Calypso could grab Phoenix and suffocate her or kill her while she was in the ocean. There was no chance I could use Alexander's sword. Phoenix would be long gone before my blade even moved.

No. There was no other way.

I shut my eyes.

All of this for nothing. Venturing into this world of hurt… for nothing.

Slowly, I set the backpack full of Roses in a waiting Doberman pinscher's mouth. Calypso, with her free hand, unzipped the pack and verified that the two Roses were inside. She placed the last Rose in the unzipped backpack and held the power of magic at her fingertips. I inched closer to them while Calypso zipped and secured the bag in her hand.

*So close, yet so far…* I thought longingly.

"Well done, boy," Calypso grinned. "Unfortunately, this girl is holding you back from your full potential. Look at what she did to you today. Look at what she did to all of Arma. Once you come work for me and my master, you cannot have her anchoring you down."

A few more inches closer.

Time slowed. My heartbeat boomed in my ears, and my breath completely stopped.

"CALYPSO, NO!"

Calypso smiled evilly. She raised the gleaming blade that shone in the sun. Phoenix's breath turned cold, regret in her gaze, sorrow in her heart.

"*NO!*" I leapt over the canines, feeling like I was moving in slow motion as the blade came down towards Phoenix's heart.

A look of shock spread on Calypso's face as I grasped the backpack and Phoenix mid-flight, shoving them into the ocean. Calypso also tumbled right behind them.

We dove into the salty bay with a huge crash.

Something made Phoenix's eyes widen, and she paddled as fast as she could towards the shore. I wasn't sure what it was, but at the moment, I didn't care.

I closed my eyes, and pushing the anger and panic aside, collected particles of oxygen, encasing Calypso in them like an air bubble.

Calypso's eyes widened.

"*Never. Hurt. Phoenix.*" I thundered, my voice echoing through the ocean water.

"You should not have done that!" Calypso yelled, her anger faltering to reveal fear. "You forget! I know you control water. Why would I have my stand-off near the ocean if I didn't have another plan?"

"Plan B?" I asked, my anger slinking away into trepidation.

Calypso laughed heinously, enjoying herself again. "Oh, look at that! Seems your friend—Phoenix, was it?—is going to die a very slow and agonizing death."

"SEAMUS!" Phoenix screamed from somewhere behind me. "HELP!"

I whipped around to find a colossal red kraken waving its tentacles in the water madly, and Phoenix desperately trying to dodge its deadly ink while staying afloat.

"PHOENIX!" I yelled.

How had a kraken come here? The evening before Phoenix and I ran away from home, when Phoenix was trying to convince me to overcome my fear of heights and jump off the sea cliff, she had said, *Are you really scared of krakens in this bay? They live in deeper waters, which you should know.*

I did know. She was right.

That's when I noticed something trailing in the water near Phoenix.

It was blood.

Calypso's plan pieced together in my head like a puzzle that finally fit into place. Calypso had planned on killing Phoenix from the very beginning, but that failed since WAD rescued us. She'd used her second play and met us here, but at the last minute, I was able to pry Phoenix from her grip again. However, she had a third plan because had she anticipated my use of the ocean. She'd lured a kraken from the deep and into the bay, and the blood from Phoenix's wounds made her an easy bait.

If I left Calypso, the oxygen would drain away and the air bubble I formed would pop.

She'd *escape*.

On the other hand, Phoenix was out there, weak and trying to fight a kraken by herself. She didn't stand a chance without my help. I wouldn't let her die. I *couldn't* let her die.

I squeezed my eyes shut. There was no real decision.

Was there ever?

"I'm sorry, Glavio," I muttered under my breath. Then I willed the ocean to carry me away from her air bubble, my concentration dissipating and her oxygen depleting.

*Go, Seamus, just go. Don't look back.*

"Seamus!" Calypso screamed, her voice already sounding gurgly.

"*DON'T LOOK BACK!*" I yelled furiously, shoving aside the pain and chaos. It took all of my willpower—walking away and letting her escape.

The woman who had hurt me so much. Who had hurt *Phoenix* so much.

Gone.

I willed the ocean to move me faster, farther away from Calypso, who desperately tried to keep afloat while paddling after me.

"PHOENIX!" I screamed.

The kraken was huge and scary. Its eye was ginormous and yellow. Its skin was puckery and thick. Its mouth had thousands of sharp, pointy teeth poking out of it, ready to kill.

"Phoenix, get to the shore!" I called. I could tell by the tortured expression on her face that the wound was tormenting her. The saltwater lapping on it was definitely not helping either.

"I won't leave you!" she strained.

"I can handle it!" I called. "Look, Phoenix, you're extremely strong and capable, but right now you're hurt. Moreover, we are in water. This is my territory. You have to get to shore and let me handle this."

Phoenix shook her head at me, unconvinced.

"I have a plan," I added.

Phoenix still looked doubtful.

The kraken roared, thrashing its tentacles, and while I was able to use the water to keep me still, Phoenix was shot through the water, almost twenty feet in the other direction.

That's when I realized Phoenix was not going to comply, and I didn't have time to argue with her.

"You can hate me for this later, Phoenix," I muttered under my breath, closing my eyes and willing the water to push Phoenix towards the shore. I didn't open my eyes until I felt the shore pushing against the ripples of the ocean.

"Seamus!" Calypso shouted.

I spun around to find Calypso, five feet away from me, grinning.

"You will regret the day you ever challenged me."

"We're in the *ocean*," I reminded her.

Before she could come up with a reply, the kraken, who was growing impatient, sped at us, its disgusting mouth open.

I, acting quickly, dove down into the ocean as fast as I could. I felt the cold skin of the kraken brush against me as it raced towards Calypso, who screamed with dread.

Through the haze of the water, I saw the kraken swallowing her whole.

I gulped.

My eyes closed as I tried to blend in with the water, racing towards the beach as fast as I could with the remainder of my energy. The beach shore approached faster and faster.

*Hurry up… hurry up… HURRY UP!*

I tried to force myself to look backwards, but my eyes froze on the path ahead of me. My mind repeated four words over and over again: *Krakens swallow people whole. Krakens swallow people whole. Krakens swallow people whole.*

*KRAKENS SWALLOW PEOPLE WHOLE!!!!!!!!!!!!!!*

A huge wave of relief swept over me when I felt the scorching sand beneath my feet. I crawled onto the beach and flopped onto my back, wheezing, exhausted.

"Seamus," Phoenix gasped from somewhere behind me. "You made it!"

"I told you," I choked, keeping my eyes on the sky, too exhausted to express any emotion. "I had a plan."

Phoenix staggered towards me. She'd ripped off a piece of her shirt and wrapped it around her stomach where her wound was. With a cut like that, it was a surprise she hadn't passed out yet.

"The Roses," I managed weakly. "They're lost. Probably broken by now."

"Nope." Phoenix grinned slightly, revealing a black backpack that held the Roses. "I checked. They're okay."

"But when the kraken hit you—how did they not break? How did you not lose the bag?"

"I held on to the bag like my life. I think the energy from the Roses made the kraken hesitate in attacking me, that's why it threw a tantrum in the water. The wave it made was strong enough to push me away from it," Phoenix told me with a grin and glinting eyes. "Also, they're a lot less fragile than we thought to begin with."

A tingling sensation bloomed inside me—a new awe and gratifying realization that we were done. And we were safe. For now.

"Phoenix," I whispered. "We did it. We saved magic."

# EIGHTEEN

**The next few moments were a blur.** Phoenix and I limped through the forest, me supporting Phoenix, who was having trouble walking. Then we put Sorin on full speed and broke through the barricade that wouldn't let us get through to Zia, much to the guards' surprise and our delight. We managed to rush Phoenix to a hospital before she passed out.

I sat on the hospital chair with the Roses next to me. One of my arms wrapped protectively around it, while the other flipped through one of the boring magazines people read when they have nothing better to do.

Phoenix's eyes slowly opened.

"Seamus?" she croaked.

I glanced up and looked at Phoenix, her head tilted slightly upwards, peering at me.

"Phoenix," I beamed, moving closer to her. "You're finally awake."

"You saved my life," Phoenix mentioned. "Twice."

I grinned.

"Thanks." She offered me a small, teasing smile. "And congrats. You finished your dare to jump off a sea cliff."

*Good old Phoenix.*

I waited for more annoying comments, but before she could, a man with black hair, a wand, and worried eyes appeared in the middle of me and Phoenix.

"Glavio?" I gaped. "What are you—"

"Come with me, quickly," Glavio hurriedly said, eyeing the backpack that was sitting on my book. I could tell he was dying to ask, but to my surprise, he stayed silent. "We need to talk somewhere private."

Phoenix frowned. "Glavio, are we going to your—"

"Not here," Glavio interrupted hastily. "Quickly. Hold on to my hand."

I was shocked and furious. We had just secured the Roses of Arma, saved all of wizarding magic, and now Phoenix was lying on a hospital bed, and Glavio hadn't even bothered to say hello, congratulate us, or ask if she was okay.

"Glavio," Phoenix asked edgily, "what's going on?"

"I'll explain everything once we get to the safe spot. A healer is waiting to help Phoenix," Glavio said.

"How did you know—" I started, but then I remembered that WAD probably stationed agents everywhere, listening and watching everything. Too bad they weren't there when we needed them most. But I knew if I mentioned this, Glavio would rant on about wizards not being allowed to meddle with prophecies.

"Hold my hand," Glavio ordered. He reached out a hand for Phoenix and me to hold. "I'm going to teleport us there, but you have to have the utmost trust and confidence in me. Do you?"

This caught me by surprise.

Trust?

I'd known Glavio for a month, but it felt like years.

"I do," Phoenix promised.

Glavio watched me with a raised eyebrow.

I nodded. That's all he needed.

I took his hand and Phoenix did the same. With his free hand, he whipped out his wand.

"Focus on me the entire way," Glavio directed. "Do not focus on anything but my hand."

Naturally, when someone says, "DO NOT THINK ABOUT TOMATOES," you think about tomatoes!

But I tried to do what he said, closing my eyes and focusing on the tingling in my fingers. I focused on my trust in Glavio, and I focused on my faith that told me he would get us to whatever safe spot he was talking about in one piece.

A whirl of motion spiraled around me, like I was doing a double front flip, jolting back into a perfect back flip, and my stomach lagging half a second every time it turned. My stomach turned up and down like I was floating in midair.

Thankfully, it was over as soon as it had started.

I grabbed on to Glavio for support as my head spun dizzily. He held me before I managed to steady myself.

Phoenix already stood, studying the landscape.

When my eyes stopped seeing stars everywhere and looked up, I immediately recognized the welcoming home. Just seeing it again brought a small grin to my face.

"We're at your house." Stars twinkled in the darkened sky.

Glavio nodded. "Come on, let's get you inside, and then I'll explain why I had to be so rash in the hospital room."

\*\*\*

A few minutes later, we were settled in Glavio's cozy living room, with blankets covering our cold feet and Glavio's sister's hot chocolate. Phoenix lay on a couch with a blanket over her and hot chocolate on the coffee table next to her.

Unfortunately, sitting in the most comfortable chair in the living room was also Hestia. Phoenix was taken inside and healed by Hestia. She was already feeling better, her pale, tinged cheeks finally gaining color.

Alright, so, begrudgingly, Hestia saved Phoenix *twice*. Even so, the rather rude healer felt like an intruder. Phoenix may have venerated her, but I still didn't like her.

While I was lost in my thoughts, Phoenix sat straight up, which was remarkable considering her injury, with her eyes wide.

"I just remembered *Sorin*!" Phoenix exclaimed, causing my eyes to widen too. That poor, dependable pegasus!

Glavio shook his head. "He's in the stables. The Wizarding Agency of Defense can do a lot more than it's given credit for."

"Except maybe save the world," I muttered under my breath. Glavio raised his eyebrows the slightest bit in my direction that no one else noticed. My cheeks flushed slightly, but he chose to ignore my comment.

"I still suspect Calypso worked for some greater cause. Her 'Master,' as she called it, could have had agents and spies anywhere around the hospital, which was why I had to rush out of there. Especially to secure the Roses."

A WAD agent had picked up the backpack containing the Roses as soon as we stepped foot inside the house. I recognized him as the driver of the carriage that had got us home, but he and Glavio did not exchange a word. He nodded at me and Phoenix before disappearing into thin air.

"I'm sorry if I came across as cold or inconsiderate." Glavio smiled wearily, although there was a twinkle in his eye.

Bags hung from under Glavio's eyes, and his back drooped slightly. He seemed like he hadn't slept for days.

Phoenix nodded.

"Now, I don't want to talk about any of this with you two just yet. We will discuss the rest of your journey later, as it is far from over." Glavio flashed his eyes at Hestia. "Could you get Phoenix situated in her room? I need to talk to Seamus for a moment."

Hestia nodded and rose to help Phoenix.

Phoenix frowned at me, and I shrugged.

"Follow me please, Seamus," Glavio ordered, leading me out of the living room and into the kitchen. I trailed behind him, and he closed the door behind me. Then he motioned for me to sit.

I dropped in the hard kitchen chair and looked up at Glavio.

Glavio studied me with a strange look that I was not used to receiving, but I was almost sure that it was—was it? —pride. Yes, there was no doubt about it. Sprinkles of pride decorated Glavio's eye.

"Glavio?" I asked uncertainly.

"Close your eyes," Glavio ordered suddenly.

"What—"

"Just trust me."

Okay…

I did trust him, now more than ever.

I closed my eyes.

"Now, I want you to focus on where Phoenix is, upstairs. You have to concentrate on her warmth. Concentrate on her fire. Once you feel that, I want you to focus on the threads. They should be warm and feel burning hot. Understand?"

My consciousness traveled to the room Phoenix was in and felt the warmth she was emitting. I envisioned the fiery threads that connected her to some sort of power source.

"Open your eyes."

I did. Glavio gazed at me intently.

"Now close your eyes again."

I frowned, but I did.

"Now feel for that magic—that power that you should have felt before. Feel for it, Seamus. Can you feel it?"

I concentrated on the warmth and magic I had felt before, and then, fighting through thick glue holding me back, I could feel the threads around me effortlessly, like I was in some sort of spider web. Each thread was a crucial part of the source, and each one as powerful as the next. It felt like I was in some sort of aura.

That's when I opened my eyes, realizing what I'd just done.

"Glavio, did I just… just…" I stuttered.

"You sensed Phoenix's aura," Glavio smiled warmly.

"Woah. It… it felt really weird. Cloudy, almost. Like I was fighting my way through some sort of thick stuff."

"Usual for beginners," Glavio explained. "As you practice more, you'll be able to sense other auras without trying."

Really?

That seemed impossible.

"But… why did you teach me that? At this moment especially?"

Glavio's face became serious. "Because you will use that at the Bridge tomorrow."

\*\*\*

"*Another* quest?" gaped Phoenix, who, by that evening, had started sitting up and even standing easily. "But we just finished our first one!"

"I know," I admitted, sitting down next to her and studying my hands, which had gotten rough over the past few days, feeling tremendously exhausted after delivering the news. Glancing back up, I said, "But Glavio said we have to. He said he's sorry, but this is our journey."

More specifically, he said *my* journey, but we both already knew that enough for me to not have to mention it.

Phoenix sighed. "Did he mention a finish line?"

I laughed softly. "I think we're a while away from the finish line." I gazed at Phoenix. "Look, Phoenix, if you don't want to go on this quest, you don't have to. Our next quest may not be as easy as this one."

Phoenix choked. "*Easy?*"

"I just mean it may be a lot more difficult than you think."

Phoenix shook her head. "It probably will be. But you seriously have to stop trying to protect me. I don't think either of us can predict what the difficulty of another quest will be. Frankly, I think we surprised Calypso and whoever she's working for. This next quest will definitely be harder." Phoenix sighed. "But, if I'm not there to help you, who will be?"

"Whoever I'm meeting on the Bridge," I told her. "Apparently they've gone on a quest too, and I have to bring them back here, where Glavio will explain everything."

"Really?" Phoenix asked. I nodded. She raised her eyebrows. "Wow, okay. That's kind of a lot to take in. But how would you even know who you're looking for?"

I shrugged. "Glavio taught me how to sense elemental auras. Apparently, the people I'm looking for have the power over elements too. I'm guessing air and earth."

Phoenix nodded. "Well, I'm still not going home. I promised you." She touched my hand.

I had to admit, I was relieved.

\*\*\*

*Dear Mom and Dad,*

*I am mailing this letter to both of you. It's only been a few days since I left, and even though it's felt like ages to me, you're probably still worried sick. I just wanted to write this letter to you to say that I'm sorry. After everything I've been through, our fight seems stupid. None of us know what's going to happen in the future. It being unknown can be really scary, but running away from it is never the answer. I know that now.*

*These past weeks have been crazy. When I ran away with Phoenix, we got kidnapped by an evil 'canine mother' who wanted me on her side, working for her (I'm not sure why) or dead. Then Glavio and the rest of WAD saved us and let us stay at Glavio's house. Glavio, a wizard, told us about a prophecy that said Phoenix and I were the ones who had to stop this evil canine mother from carrying out her plans and stealing the Roses of Arma. He trained and prepared us for our journey. We succeeded, but Phoenix got hurt. She's okay now, and so am I.*

*I know that's a lot to take in, but there's more. My journey isn't over. Phoenix and I have to go to the Bridge to meet two people with elemental powers and go on another quest with them. Right now, that's all I know. But Phoenix and I have agreed that it's our problem now. It's up to us to save the world.*

*I'm sorry, but I will not be living with you anytime soon. I will be traveling on journeys and staying at Glavio's house when I'm not. I need to do this.*

*I hope you both are well and I'm really sorry if I scared you. Believe it or not, I love you guys more than either of you ever knew. Please take care.*

*Yours truly,*

*Seamus*

\*\*\*

The next day, when I woke up and hurried down the stairs, Phoenix was already in the kitchen with another pile of whipped cream for breakfast. I grinned and sat down next to her.

"Good morning, Seamus," Glavio greeted, flipping an omelet in the air. "I hope you slept well."

"That bed was great before, and it was even better now. I felt like I hadn't had a real good night's sleep for weeks," I admitted pleasantly. Glavio smiled, but I was too busy frowning at the two bags on the countertop to acknowledge it. "What are the bags for?"

"You two," Glavio explained, sipping a steaming cup of coffee.

"We're leaving right away?" Phoenix asked, noticeable disappointment in her eyes.

Glavio nodded, mixing sugar into his coffee while purposefully not looking at our faces. "I know it's sudden, but this is something you have to do. I'm going to teleport you two there, but I can't help you once you're on the Bridge."

"Why not?" I asked.

"It's too much for you to understand right now, but once you return, I will explain everything. I think you should leave once you're finished with your breakfast."

Phoenix spooned some more whipped cream. "What are you not telling us, Glavio? Right from the start, you've been keeping something from us. You aren't exactly hard to read."

Glavio shook his head. "All will be explained. You must hurry."

I didn't have much of an intention to rush another never-ending whipped cream bottle, but I could tell, just by looking into Glavio's eyes, that this was important. *Very* important. Still, I enjoyed every bite of my waffles until they were done.

Glavio stared at us, waiting for us to finish.

I glanced at Phoenix, who was licking the last of her whipped cream off of her fork. I rolled my eyes. *Phoenix*, I thought, shaking my head.

"Good, you're finished." Glavio whipped his wand and our plates disappeared. The crumbs that had spilled (mostly me, since Phoenix seemed to have just eaten whipped cream) were magically cleaned up. "Now, take your bags."

Phoenix and I exchanged looks, but we rose from our seats and took the bags that were set on the table. They were surprisingly light.

"What's in these?" I questioned, half expecting Glavio to stay silent.

"Money and some basic travel needs," he answered. "Just in case you decide to stop somewhere to talk before coming back."

"Why would we—"

"You'll understand later. Now hold on to me. Yes, perfect. Okay, you're going to feel the same thing you felt before. Brace yourself."

I squeezed my eyes shut, remembering how unpleasant teleportation had been the first time, not exactly excited to relive the jolting and turns that my stomach would take.

All of a sudden, we were shoved into a portal. My stomach aced its acrobatics, and the ground seemed to jolt left and right underneath my feet. But this time, it felt more like an echo. This time, when my eyes were closed, I could focus on my faith in Glavio. I focused on his strength.

But was that really all there was to Glavio?

He'd kept so many things from us.

I tried not to focus on his secrets, but I couldn't help myself.

# NINETEEN

**We were whizzed out of the dizziness** into a dark alleyway. I hit the ground with a lot of force, and Phoenix slammed into the ground next to me. Glavio groaned a few feet away from me.

I managed to prop myself up with my arms, stars popping in my corneas. My eyes adjusted to the darkness of the alleyway we were in as I moaned woozily.

"This doesn't look like the Bridge," Phoenix groaned.

"Nice observation, genius," I remarked, shaking my head fiercely.

"Hey, I was just hit in the head by a brick wall, and I can hardly see what's in front of me." Phoenix rubbed her eyes. "Why were we teleported here? Speaking of which, where's Glavio?"

"Right here," replied Glavio, standing up and brushing himself off. His eyes were a beacon of hurt. "Why… who broke their… their faith in me?" he asked softly.

A pang of guilt, like spikes in the back of my skull, stabbed at me torturously.

That look on his face. It was beating me up.

"I'm sorry, Glavio." I said quietly, standing up. "It… it was me."

Glavio looked like he'd just been punched. It was the first time I'd seen such a pure, undisguised reaction from him, and it killed me. "Why did you do that? You… you told me you trusted me. Didn't you… didn't you trust me when I was teleporting you out of the hospital?".

"I did, Glavio… but at the hospital, we'd just come back from a quest. Phoenix was hurt. It was a relief to see you. It was just an instant decision and…" My voice trailed off.

"So… you don't actually trust me?"

"I… no, well…" I sighed. "It's just, from the very beginning, it's felt like you've been keeping something from us. Hiding something. And after all we've been through, you still seem… secretive. I'm sorry, Glavio, I really am. I just can't trust you forever without… some answers."

"He's right." Phoenix rose from the ground and looked at Glavio. "It seems wrong, somehow. And… I may have broken my faith, too. So, it probably wasn't all him." She sighed, but I was grateful for the support.

Glavio dropped down on the cobblestone floor. "I should have known you'd want answers."

"Yeah… you kinda should've," Phoenix admitted. "But you've done a lot for us, Glavio."

She didn't have to go on. Her message was clear: *We're willing to give you the chance to explain because it's you, Glavio. Please take it.*

There was a long pause.

"Okay." Glavio took a deep breath and rose from the ground. "Centuries ago, a prophecy was issued. It was about water and air. But having elemental powers is very rare. It took a while for a girl, born from air, to show up, and a boy, born from water, to show up. Immediately, WAD knew they were the ones of the prophecy. Unfortunately, so did others. Others who wanted to hurt them.

"It was against wizarding code for wizards to meddle with prophecies—for wizards to meddle with fate. The boy showed up on my doorstep. It was hard for him to accept his fate, but he did. He succeeded in his first quest, but now it is time for him to meet the other—the girl born from air."

"Wait…" I closed my eyes. "There's a prophecy about me and this girl with the power over air?"

Glavio nodded and cleared his throat.

*"One of riches, the other of rags*

*Each of them from different flags*

*Water and Air*

*together, apart*

*Up against the shadow's art*

*Many challenges they shall face,*

*Either fall with regret or fall with grace*

*Neither choice is right*

*Triumph with the side of darkness*

*Or risk it all in the final fight."*

There was a long, extended moment of silence.

The words of the prophecy twirled in my head over and over again. *One of riches, the other of rags. Each of them from different flags. Water and air, together apart.* Together apart? Did that mean I'd met this girl before? *Up against the shadow's art.* That sent a shiver down my spine. As for the rest of the prophecy, I couldn't even begin to think about it. Especially the last two lines, which I carefully avoided dealing with.

Phoenix hushed. Finally, she got the courage to speak. "Seamus, are you sure you want to—"

"Let's go," I interrupted.

Glavio considered me with a look of surprise. I nodded at him.

"It's clear me and whoever this girl is are the only ones who can save Arma. So, we have to do it." I turned to Phoenix. "I know you're sick of me asking this, but this prophecy changes everything. Do you still want to—"

Phoenix inhaled sharply and nodded. "Yes."

I glanced sideways at Glavio. "Take us to the Bridge."

Glavio smiled. "Thank you," he whispered. "Focus on your trust." Then he took our hands, and we rushed into another world of motion.

This time, teleporting seemed like muscle memory, and my insides stayed steady as the portal took over.

We were spat out of the motion into a crowded square. Without a second to spare, I let go of Glavio's hand and squinted through the hurrying people. The Bridge glowed in the golden light of the sunrise, and the outline of the Seer's house stood bold against the crimson sky.

"Go," Glavio nodded. "Find them."

With one last glance at Glavio, Phoenix and I swam through the crowd of people, navigating our way to the Bridge.

"Start looking for her aura," Phoenix advised. "This crowd is too thick to actually find her."

I closed my eyes and searched for the source of power I had felt from Phoenix before. I searched for the wind in the threads and the magic of air shooting through the aura. I searched for the spider web envisioned before.

A spark of magic ignited somewhere in the crowd. Its threads of power tugged on me. My eyes flew open.

"This way!" I called, pointing in the direction the aura hovered. "I can feel it!"

Phoenix raced behind me as I bolted through the crowds, keeping the string of magic within range. Soon it was so close, I could feel its element buzzing inside me.

I squinted through the crowd, searching for where the power was strongest. The hum of the source thrummed in my ears, its magic beating inside of me. I closed my eyes, concentrating, and then opened them again.

"Follow me!" I called to Phoenix, taking off through the crowd once again. I screeched to a stop, Phoenix almost running straight into me.

"Have you found her?" Phoenix asked, breathing hard and bending over on her knees.

I nodded and pointed. In the middle of the crowd was a girl with wavy, dirty blonde hair that reached past her shoulders. She had deep, sky blue eyes, which held experience and strength. Her skin was pale and pearly. Freckles dotted her nose, and her fingers were long and nimble. Next to her stood a boy. His skin was slightly lighter than Phoenix's. His grey eyes were alert and ready. He had calloused hands and long legs. He was a little taller than the girl, and when I closed my eyes, I could feel an elemental aura bouncing off him too.

Air and earth.

"You see that girl over there? Next to that boy?" I nudged Phoenix.

Phoenix squinted through the crowd of people. "Yeah, I see her." Her eyes widened in understanding. "So, *she's* the…"

I fixated on her. "Let's go meet them."

We sauntered through the crowd. The boy, who noticed us first, prodded the girl, who frowned at us. They hovered in their spots as we pushed through the crowd towards them, watching us with calculating eyes.

When we reached them, the boy asked, "Do I know you?"

I took a deep breath. "Not yet, but I'm Seamus, and this is Phoenix. Glavio, a WAD agent, sent us. He wants us to take you to his house… and he has an explanation."

Phoenix rolled her eyes. Okay, I really needed to work on my people skills. It'd be a surprise if they didn't assume we were hustling them.

The girl frowned at the boy, mouthed something I couldn't make out, and then turned to us. "We know who Glavio is."

"Wait, you *know* Glavio?" Phoenix clamored. "How do you *know* Glavio?"

The girl checked with the boy, and he shrugged. Then she observed us carefully. "He helped us in a spot of trouble. He took us in, gave us a home for a bit, and sent us off on our journey."

Phoenix and I exchanged looks.

"But…" I squeezed my hands against my forehead. "He made it sound like he never met you when he told us the prophecy. Are you saying he lied again?"

"Lied about what?" the boy pressed. "Who are you? How does Glavio know you?"

I shook my head. "I'm sorry, can we pause for a moment? Who are *you*?"

The girl stepped forward. "My name is Skyler, and this is Jax Miller. I think… we were supposed to meet you on the Bridge."

# ACKNOWLEDGMENTS

There are MANY people who contributed to this book. Some helped it long before it even started! Authoring *Roses of Arma* was most definitely not a one-person job. I don't know if I'll be able to mention everyone here, so I am really sorry if I miss you.

First of all, I want to thank my friends from SCT for all of the much-needed support and encouragement. That crew is simply the best! From strings of emails (which were technically not allowed during classes, but they didn't let that stop them) to designing book covers and long talks that took up most of our break time, they were the first ROA fans! A special shout-out to Reagan and Sudha, who were among my first readers and supporters when few people were willing to read my book. I am lucky to have such amazing friends who practically snatched the manuscript out of my hands! A big thanks to Samara for being my first hard-core editor. She spent an enormous amount of time editing, revising, pointing out plot holes, and giving me feedback on my writing. Her wisdom is salt and pepper in this soup. Your input was very much appreciated!

I want to thank Nya, who was my partner in crime. She spent time with me molding the plot and characters, laughing at stupid jokes, baking terrible cakes, and playing online Uno. We spent hours together using our imagination to get ourselves out of ridiculous jams in ROA. If my characters got tied up in a situation they couldn't get out of, she'd swoop in, and we'd work out a solution together. It took an unimaginable amount of time and effort getting this book to where it is now, and she was there through all of that, shouldering the workload of this dream with me.

I want to thank my teacher, Mrs. Crowder, for encouraging me in every possible way. Thank you, Ms. Crowder, for cheering me on and telling me that once I published a book, you'd want the first copy. It boosted me up and encouraged me to finally finish a novel. The 'Best Writer of the Year' award you gave me meant a lot. Thank you so much. Without you, this book probably wouldn't exist!

This is a weird one, but I couldn't leave my dog out of it. She's been the source of everlasting love and encouragement. Thank you, Laila!

I also want to thank my family. Many thanks to my dad, who was one of the few people who took my book in hand and spent hours on it, editing, discussing, revising, plot-tightening, making phone calls, finding other authors for me to talk to—the list is never-ending. He was one of the few people who took my needy, flawed book head on. His ideas and feedback have transformed my manuscript into a novel! Thanks to my marvelous mom and brilliant brother, whose love I cherish the most. My grandparents were supporters from the very start, and all of my family in India encouraged me to get this book published and keep on writing. I could not have finished this novel without them by my side. Thanks to my aunt, Pallavi, who designed the first hardcover for *Roses of Arma*, and to everybody in India who helped print my manuscript. My excitement when I first saw a hard copy of my book is something only an author can fully understand.

I also want to thank my best friend, who pushed me forward when I wasn't sure I could write anymore and held me up through all my troubles. I'm extremely lucky to have her. Even after my writing took a pause, with our long talks and stupid jokes, she managed to get me back into it. When I told her I had doubts as to whether my book would make it or not, she screamed at me in all caps until I said, "Okay, okay! I didn't mean to make you mad!" She was demanding! Thank you so much, my BFF. I hope you know that I wouldn't be writing this without you.

Lastly, I want to specially thank my grandfather. He read my book, front to back, and spent his valuable time doing whatever he could to publish it. He made an *abundance* of phone calls and had many conversations with people until my uncle, Rakesh Jain, pointed him in the direction of our publisher. He negotiated a deal with them and promised me my book would be out there in the world before I knew it. He carried through and fulfilled my dream. His love is one of the best things I have in this world. I love you indescribably, Grandpa, and thank you for everything you have done for me and for the *Roses of Arma*.

Thank you all.

Naisha Randhar

Made in the USA
Monee, IL
14 September 2023